PRAISE FOR *IN CERTAIN CIRCLES*

'Less malignant than *The Watch Tower*, *In Certain Circles* is no less psychologically profound. Rather, its quietude and graceful turning of the screws bring it all the more closer to a kind of truth.' Jessica Au, *Guardian*

'Like the rest of [Harrower's] work, the novel is severely achieved: the coolly exact prose cannot be distinguished from the ashen exhaustion of its tragic fires...The book belongs with her best work, with *The Watch Tower* and *The Long Prospect*.' James Wood, *New Yorker*

'*In Certain Circles* displays the qualities that won Harrower the admiration of Patrick White and Christina Stead...This is high-style psychological realism of the most mature kind.' Owen Richardson, *Sunday Age*

'A coup...Weirdly thrilling line by line...[The novel's] dense and adult conversation crackles with a sense of moral urgency.' Delia Falconer, *Australian*

'[Harrower's] insights into the nature of love, the role of women and the torsions of power in even the most ordinary relationship are bitter and sometimes cruel...Yet they are always delivered via the honeyed dipper of her prose.' Geordie Williamson, *Monthly*

'Whatever the reason behind her decision not to allow this novel to be released four decades ago, its rebirth is an event to be celebrated.' Andrew Riemer, *Sydney Morning Herald*

ELIZABETH HARROWER was born in Sydney in 1928. She lived in Newcastle until her family moved back to Sydney when she was eleven.

In 1951 Harrower travelled to London and began to write. Her first novel, *Down in the City*, was published there in 1957 and was followed by *The Long Prospect* a year later. In 1959 she returned to Sydney, where she worked in radio and then in publishing. Her third novel, *The Catherine Wheel*, appeared in 1960.

Harrower published *The Watch Tower* in 1966. Four years later she finished a new novel, *In Certain Circles*, but withdrew it from publication at the last moment, in 1971. It remained unpublished until 2014.

In Certain Circles is Harrower's final completed novel, though in the 1970s and 1980s she continued to write short fiction. She is one of the most important postwar Australian writers. She was admired by many of her contemporaries, including Patrick White and Christina Stead, who both became lifelong friends. Her novels are now being acclaimed by a new generation of readers and writers.

Elizabeth Harrower lives in Sydney.

IN CERTAIN CIRCLES

ELIZABETH HARROWER

TEXT PUBLISHING
MELBOURNE AUSTRALIA

textpublishing.com.au

The Text Publishing Company
Swann House
22 William Street
Melbourne Victoria 3000
Australia

First published in 2014 by The Text Publishing Company
This edition published in 2015

Typeset in Centaur MT by J & M Typesetting
Book design by W.H. Chong
Printed and bound in Australia by Griffin Press, an Accredited ISO AS/NZS 14001:2004 Environmental Management System printer

National Library of Australia Cataloguing-in-Publication entry:

Author: Harrower, Elizabeth, 1928–

Title: In certain circles / Elizabeth Harrower.

ISBN: 9781922182968 (paperback)

ISBN: 9781925095272 (ebook)

Dewey Number: A823.4

PART ONE

'I hear Russell laughing.' His mother spoke in a troubled, haunted tone.

Zoe moved instantly from her chair to sit on the rail of the verandah. She looked across the garden to the tennis court where four figures ran to the net and paused, arguing some fine point of order.

'That's not so unusual. He laughs quite often. He makes me laugh often.' It was impossible not to smile. Zoe adored him. But her mother's unnecessary grief did make her feel embarrassed: she had no talent for this sort of thing. After all, he was alive—unlike many of his friends. He was home from wars and in one piece. Having done history for matriculation, Zoe knew, and thought her mother might not realise as fully, that men had always been coming home from wars. It was more natural to rejoice.

Certainly (she gazed in sudden depression at the four now

running backwards to the corners of the court, like figures attached to a maypole), certainly, the papers had for weeks and months been printing horrible facts, terrible facts. For a while, she hid the newspapers, and everyone was irritated and mystified and blamed a neighbour's dog, a cocker spaniel famous for such depredations. Then, suddenly, they stopped talking about the dog, so Zoe knew that she had been seen, and gave up. Newspapers were awkward to dispose of, anyway. For a week or so of warm weather she was always going for walks, one arm held stiff against her side, sweating gently all over inside an enveloping coat.

Over her shoulder, Zoe glanced at her mother with apprehension. For the years he was gone, perhaps dead, she had outwardly altered little. When he was restored to her, and her worst imaginings were not only publicly confirmed but outstripped, she aged, fading visibly, as if some inner stiffening, some secret resource had quite disappeared. She was quieter, paler, powdered over. Everybody noticed. Zoe felt it was not like her, to be seen to be shaken. It made her seem weaker, and mortal. Zoe was surprised and resentful. Now, against her hand, she could feel the warm stone of a supporting pillar of the verandah. She had been born in this house.

Down on the court, the game continued. Mrs Howard eyed the distant antics with the dismay of a one-time A-grade player.

'Your poor father,' she murmured. 'They probably think they're doing him a favour. I don't think I can bear to watch.'

Having restored his family to life by returning alive,

Russell had proceeded to alarm and disappoint his parents by refusing to involve himself in any of the activities they felt him suited to. So he took up a racquet almost before his father was aware of needing a game.

'*You* might have played instead of that little girl. At least you have some idea.' Mrs Howard rose from the low bamboo chair. 'I'll get some cold drinks. That will give them an excuse to stop.'

'But it's so hot. I'd get burnt.' Zoe touched her pale cheek. 'Anna's fair, too.'

'She probably goes brown, just the same. A lot of fair people do.' Zoe yawned and slid her fingers again across her smooth white face. '*Nobody* plays tennis any more. You could have an Olympic pool down there. I wish you would.'

This had been said before.

'Be nice, if they come up while I'm in the kitchen. You know Anna's a little orphan.'

Zoe gave an indescribable sound of disgust. She rolled her head about, seeming quite unable to recover. 'A little orphan! Anyway, if she is, so is her brother, and you can't pretend *he's* pathetic.' In one beautiful, impulsive movement she was at her mother's side by the door, smiling into her eyes, eager, appealing, high-spirited but meaning no harm, teasing but vulnerable. 'Why didn't *you* have a game?' Her voice was soft, almost caressing.

'I get breathless.'

'Do you want any help? Should I bring out the drinks? You sit down.'

'It's all in my mind, what I want to do. I'll call if I need you.' Mrs Howard looked at her daughter with admiration and love, patted her shoulder and went inside.

Zoe lay down again, staring across the garden, past the camphor laurels, to the place where her father, her brother, and her brother's two new-found orphans ran about in the sun. Whether the expressions so recently shown on her face belonged to the luminous quality of her eyes, or to the shape of her mouth, or to her nature, neither Zoe nor her mother yet knew: she was only seventeen.

Zoe had wakened in this square stone house on the north side of Sydney Harbour, and learned soon afterwards from her family and their friends that she was remarkable. There was a big garden. There were people of her own size for company. At the end of the short street of old houses in long-established gardens was a white curved beach with rocks, rock pools, very small waves, shells, pebbles, fine sand. She swam before she walked.

Once, on a school tour to view relics of old colonial days, a girl carved her initials on the smoke-darkened stool in the ante-room of a courthouse: they were queuing to enter the cells and inspect the irons clamped on the necks and legs of convicts in another world, in a fiction they disbelieved entirely.

The pupil with the knife was pounced on. 'Ah! Patricia has just reassured future generations about the date of her visit. They'll be *so* interested. An outstanding girl like Patricia.' The girl mumbled. Her companions brooded. The teacher, much tried, told them, 'You're nonentities, that's what you are.'

Could anything be worse? Especially when it was not even true.

Zoe was one of those whose parents were referred to in newspapers and magazines as 'well-known identities'. Her mother and father were biologists, and had written textbooks and others for the general reader which had been published overseas. They had travelled. They were invited to join public discussion groups. They were interviewed and photographed, and were on the list of those whose opinions on every subject from crime to mayonnaise were expected to be of interest to the whole city.

Mrs Howard was a useful example of a woman who combined a successful career with a happy home life. Whenever such a phenomenon needed illustration, journalists and producers were as likely to think of Alice Howard as anyone else in town.

If you could believe what you read, Sydney was one of the largest cities in the English-speaking world. In this place—Sydney—then, that the newspapers of the city were always praising, Zoe's mother and father held moderately conspicuous positions; knew everyone; knew where to go for what and whom to see; knew who was the leader in each particular field; knew how to ask and grant favours. Now from these very parents who were regarded by strangers as quite special, Zoe had learned that she surpassed them in all things just because she was herself. She and Russell were greatly taken notice of. Russell was never affected by the propaganda, having a life of his own from the start; Zoe took attention and praise for granted, as though they were part of the public utilities, like running water and electricity. She was quite sated with the interest turned on her, but did not think it unjustified.

World-weary as any international success, so confident that few opinions could move her, fearless, seventeen, she watched the three amateurs massacre her father's nerves down on the court.

Her father. Clive Howard. Dr Howard. He should have been a farmer. He had a rural sort of face. He looked at home, leaning on a hoe. Her mother was contented in the country, on holidays, taking a batch of scones from an old fuel stove, playing pioneers. They stayed with distant relations on a sheep station hundreds of miles from the city. Her father rode. Her mother gardened and gossiped. It was like a luxurious camp in a desert, but they fitted in, not seeming artificial there. Out in the bush, their city lives were like roles thrust on them accidentally, roles that made them unconsciously sigh. They were nice, and able and accomplished, but innocent, Zoe thought, and knew nothing much about anything real compared with Russell. Except worms or starfish or flies.

Of course, uxorious described them, too. Uxorious. Zoe recognised that her own life was harmonious partly because of it, but for some years she had felt the pressure of a too warm and close parental interest in her future as a lover. Their prospective delight intruded on her sense of herself as a private person. Like voyeurs, she thought, sensing their wish to advise, to be present, to take part almost.

'Zo! I can't get past.' Holding a tray, Mrs Howard stood at the side of her supine and apparently unconscious daughter.

'Oh!' Long chairs scattered about barricaded off one half of the verandah. Contrite, Zoe took the heavy tray over to the table, eyeing the glasses, ice, fruit juice and various bottles. 'I was thinking about parents and orphans.' She flashed a smile across her shoulder: while in passivity her face, with its light grey eyes and fine bone structure, was more than pleasing, in animation it could be beautiful. Her smile was always astonishing, causing the recipient to pause and inwardly acknowledge that some boon or blessing had unexpectedly been granted. So her mother paused briefly now, never having grown used to these dazzlingly varied and unpremeditated glances.

'You only think of orphans in fairy tales.' Zoe straightened the glasses on the tray. 'Wandering in, hand in hand out of the woods, all misty and neglected and bedraggled. I've never met one before.'

'That's not to say they don't exist,' her mother pointed out. 'When I think of some of my students, I realise that you lead a very sheltered life.'

'*I* do?' Zoe gave an incredulous laugh. The captain of the school, editor of the paper, with the staff leaning heavily on her. Did they suppose she was given those marks out of pure philanthropy? And what about sailing? Had she not won more races there on the harbour than any girl of her age? She was a concert-goer. She could handle a movie camera with some skill, and a car better than her father. She could cook. With the few boys who had an interest in politics she had attended meetings of every shade, and been introduced by print to the prophets and their disciples. She had read millions of books. Although

7

she was fortunate and wanted nothing, of her own accord, from childhood, she had noticed poverty when she saw it in the streets. Mentally, she had dealt with it all. Abracadabra! Misery abolished! In her imagination, as something between a game and a duty, people and buildings were transformed. Now she was older and transformations were harder. But she had helped to raise money for charity, and with a church group she had visited old people in their own homes for a few weeks or months two or three years ago. Virtue on virtue! Then there was the loss of Russell for that long time, when he was everything, so important to her.

'*I* lead a sheltered life?' she repeated on a vaguer note. 'When I never stop doing things, and after all you say about your students.'

'Call them, Zo, before the ice melts and everything's lukewarm.'

Zoe did, with some restraint.

'I meant,' Mrs Howard sat down and brushed some loose hair away from her face, 'compared with Russell or the orphans.'

'Oh, well. Russell and that man, they're older. I'll be different then, too.' Though not in a war, not a prisoner, not knowing about tortures and starvation, she could but hope. Yet even while he was her age and younger, experience had touched Russell—a serious illness, and the death of his two closest friends. One autumn day, swimming from a deserted beach, the three boys were caught in a strong rip and swept out past the headland. A freak wave washed Russell unconscious on to the rocks, and a fisherman rescued him. The bodies of the other boys were never found. Zoe was told what had happened. All that was real was what she had witnessed: Russell's shock, Russell's grief.

'Here they come.' Mrs Howard began to fill the glasses. When she felt ill, as lately she had, she saw the doctor and told no one. She was by nature imperturbable, and frowned on undue sensitivity as neurotic, in poor taste. She was resolute in preserving in all circumstances a smooth social surface, and saw no reason to change because she might be less than well. At this moment, she set about the business of making Russell's rather forbidding friend, Stephen Quayle, and Stephen's young sister, at home, watching them as they walked up out of the garden across the flagstones. Bright pink oleander petals lay in a semi-circle under the trees as though reflected there. Strong winds had knocked the flowers about in the night.

Chairs and glasses were distributed. Borrowed sandshoes were removed. Mr Howard emptied his glass in one draught, then bared his exceptionally fine teeth in a smile. 'The Marx brothers could have learned something watching that game. Ah, well. At least he's giving us a daughter-in-law who knows what's what. Lily's like a rocket. Do you know her?'

'They'll meet soon. See that slate roof down through the trees?' From the verandah wall, Russell pointed. 'That's Lily's house. She's seeing some students this afternoon, or she would have been here.'

Turning to Anna, who was seated next to her, and whose fair skin, Zoe noticed, *had* burned out on the court, Zoe explained, 'Lily's a lecturer. German. Though she's so young.

She's like a fireworks display.'

And because she saw she should have played instead of this fifteen-year-old orphan with the grave eyes suitable to her fabled position in life, and because Anna would probably have liked sitting up on the shady verandah with Mrs Howard getting some sort of mother fixation (which her mother, Zoe felt certain, would have been only too happy to induce), she smiled with particular attention at the younger girl, before perceiving that her mixed intentions were observed. Although Anna was shy, and nervous, and silent, her look was none of those things. Her eyes reminded Zoe of someone. Her dress and shoes were cheap-looking and worn: she had no idea what suited her. These signs of want were repellent to Zoe. I lead a sheltered life, she thought, and then on impulse said, 'Come and see us again. We'll go out in the boat, or go to the pictures.'

With another slight shock, Zoe saw that the girl was inclined, without reproach, to disbelieve this invitation. And why shouldn't she? Zoe wondered, sipping icy pineapple juice. I've often said things without meaning them. Often I don't mean what I say. For a moment she felt chastened by she hardly knew what. Then she resisted the sinking and doubt. After all, when she said these spontaneous charming things it was rather in the nature of practice, as someone might work at a language, or diving, as if there were no limit to the excellence he might achieve. Everything she said was experimental in that way. There was the sense of being an explorer, travelling out, extending herself again and again, finding no obstacle to stand in her way. These shapeless, exciting impressions sped through her mind, and the great sense of her own never-ending possibilities brought a sudden joy. No, she was not just superficial! She did mean what she said. She would be nice, would be kind to this younger girl whose life was obviously so much less privileged than her own.

Zoe's parents had been talking to Stephen and finding him unforthcoming. Marginally aware of this, Zoe now felt her mother and father on the brink of deciding that Anna might be a more responsive subject. Chairs were hitched closer to hers. With professional ease, they moved in, questioning her about her school. Marmalade, the cat, arrived and was a momentary diversion from the strain of receiving so much adult attention—a new and exhausting experience, it was clear. Zoe listened inattentively, bored by any education but her own. The telephone rang and Mr Howard disappeared till lunch time.

Russell and his friend were talking vehemently at the far end of the verandah. The friend looked like an anarchist, or a music student, Zoe decided. A bush of tightly waving, light-brown, uncontrollable-looking hair was mostly responsible for this impression, but his tallness and thinness and fairness, the spectacles he put on and took off with long thin fingers contributed. And his eyes, the glance they gave, were positively frightening. Where did Russell pick these people up?

So far, she had noticed, this Stephen seemed—when her parents tried to talk to him—nervous, edgy, with reserves of anger, like someone too full of pressing thought to have time for conversation. Those striking golden-coloured eyes would rarely meet anyone else's. In fact, had he looked directly at anyone but Russell? Once or twice he had actually answered her father with quite alarming impatience and irritability. He was like a weird, irascible character out of some dense Russian novel.

Unexpectedly, he had laughed while Zoe observed from a distance, half-burying her face in her slippery cold glass, and she had received an impression of a gong having been sounded on a note both loud and flat. Unused to anything so discordant, she found it oddly stimulating. Uneasy, but curious, but interested, she studied this other orphan. Poor boy, she thought, accustomed to hearing her mother talk of poor boys. Privation. That was what they made you think of, he and Anna. But he was scruffy, not so entirely to-the-last-atom clean as Anna was. Her mother would put his privation look down to sex starvation, but then she put everything down to that. If you knew so surely that that was the answer to all human problems, Zoe thought, it certainly left loads of time for solving the rest. Jarred by the patness and predictability of this diagnosis, Zoe had learned to remark, 'How happy prostitutes must be! And how well balanced!'

'How many prostitutes have you ever seen?' her mother asked.

'I'm not blind.'

Now, clicking her fingernails against the empty glass she still held, with Mrs Howard's voice in the background enslaving Anna, she continued to watch Stephen. She looked at his halo of hair, at the neat shape of his ears; one was transparent in the sun and she saw his flowing blood.

Another ringing inside the house, then her father's call: 'Russell! Lily wants you.'

Russell was at the door. 'Zoe, come and talk to Stephen. Keep him company instead of posing there.'

Smiling because he knew her, knew what she was like, even to the extent of penetrating her extremely natural-looking poses that she was hardly conscious of herself, Zoe went over to sit beside Stephen Quayle.

'What do you do?' she asked, almost laughing, radiant. It never mattered what she said to men: they liked her to say anything.

'I'm a salesman.'

'Oh!' She was disliked. She was disapproved of. He had not looked at her surface at all. She was a rude child who had addressed a visiting bishop by his Christian name. 'What do you sell?' she persisted.

'Packing materials. Packing tape. Brown paper. Corrugated cardboard.'

Her fault, apparently! Avoiding the space where his face was, her glance darted about. 'Probably that's very interesting, meeting different people all the time.'

As she spoke, she had an impression of something not pleasant happening to her, something irreversible and magical and inevitable. An enchanted padlock was being fitted to her mind, and there was no key. She had met the first man ever to judge her. That he chose to do it gave him the authority, made him unquestionably her superior. She felt at some level that an essential element, necessary to her very life, had been given to her just in time. If he had not looked at that instant, said those particular words, she might not have survived another hour.

'Extremely interesting,' he agreed. 'I walk about the city and suburbs with a briefcase full of advertising samples, and wait in smelly offices for head clerks. An hour's nothing. Then he'll tell one of the juniors: "Get rid of him. I don't want anything this month."'

His anger! Zoe could think of nothing to say.

'You're looking at my shoes,' he said.

'I am not looking at your shoes.' Zoe suddenly stared at them.

'Ordinary soles wear out too fast. I get a bootmaker to fix that extra leather.' He turned his right foot sideways, and frowned. 'I didn't wear them on the court.'

Zoe dared to glance at his face, though his look acted on her nerves like an electric shock. 'I don't care if you wear them in the bath,' she said indignantly. As if she had nothing better to do than worry about his shoes! He must think I'm a fetishist, she thought. Or was it only men who were?

He was looking out at the massed trees, the glimpses of water, the dense shadows and blazing greens, under the enormous empty sky. 'Like the Botanic Gardens. You're lucky.' Stretching in the cushioned chair and staring away from so much brilliant colour to the white-painted ceiling, he said, 'Human beings were never born to be salesmen or clerks.'

'What were they born to be?' Zoe asked, bemused. None of the boys she knew ever made remarks like that. 'What are you going to do afterwards? I mean—when you stop this?'

'This is what I do.'

Zoe said nothing. He was superior to her, quite possibly the only person in the world who was, since he was the only person who had so far claimed to be, therefore, what he said was impossible. Someone superior to Zoe could not conceivably spend his life as a salesman. She remembered her lessons. Somehow, he had been denied a fair chance. Men like this were ripe for communism. 'Ripe' was the word always used. She asked him.

The angry golden eyes flickered. 'How old are you?'

She told him, adding, 'We did *Utopia* last year.'

'Did you like it?'

'If you haven't read it recently, there's no point in discussing it.' Having shown that she, too, knew how to be crushing, she said, 'Why do you do this then, if you hate it so much?'

He sighed, forgetting her, and rubbed a thin hand up and down his chest, then stopped to feel the buttons on his shirt, in some private despair, the witnessing of which pierced Zoe's mind.

'I do it'—still he held a shirt button between forefinger and thumb—'I suppose I do it to exist. For this shirt. For a roof and food. To have hair cut and teeth filled. To pay bus fares to go to the office to make money to exist.'

Zoe felt stunned and persecuted meeting someone like this in real life. 'What about Anna?'

'Anna. I suppose she'll turn into one of those clerks, working to eat. She'll meet other clerks, and might marry one.'

Noticing her bare legs stretched out in front of her, feeling them looked at, Zoe tugged at her short shorts. 'You probably make it sound much drearier than it is.' Maybe this was his sort of joke, like British understatement in reverse. It was so feeble to be in a weak position and complain. 'Couldn't either of you get scholarships? Can't your relations and friends do something?'

His face looked suddenly very tired. His whole attitude was one of exhaustion. Yet twenty-three, though moderately old, was not old.

Turning abruptly, Zoe called to her mother, 'Should I ask Mrs Perkins about lunch?'

Mrs Howard received the signal of distress. 'Anna and I are going in. We'll call you in a minute.'

So Zoe laboured along with her brother's friend. 'What were you and Russell talking about when he went away?

Stephen smiled. 'Relativity. Have you done that?'

She gave him a glance full of aversion. She had never been baited, never been blamed for the state of the world, never been scorned like this. A flash of apricot fur caught her eye. 'There's Marmalade digging up the garden. I'll have to go. Don't come into the sun unless you want to.'

From the scraping sound of his chair behind her as she ran down the steps, he wanted to. But the relief of escaping from him! Already Marmalade had vanished, but two of her mother's new plants, whatever they were, had been mangled. She pressed them back into the earth and spread out their wilting leaves. Well, she would keep this creature in the sun till he collapsed, if he followed her, even if it meant getting sunburnt herself. Hearing him approach over the grass, she turned reluctantly, and they watched each other till he reached her side.

'I've seen you somewhere,' he said. 'Or a photograph.'

Zoe thought dully, staring at him, trying to gauge the nature of this new attack. 'A month ago I won a competition. There was a photograph in the *Herald*. Or at a party or something.' She trailed off. She couldn't imagine him scanning the social pages, and the winning of competitions clearly had no interest for the gallant Stephen.

'Probably it.'

They sauntered back towards the house, breathing the moist, salty, scented air.

'Your visitors, Zoe!' Russell came down to meet them, and she ran off ahead, saying, 'I'd forgotten. I'm going out for lunch.'

Dinah and Tony and Philip stood about talking to Mr and Mrs Howard. Dinah was a friend from school. The young men were law students, and famous as football players. Zoe heard Russell explaining this to Stephen as she joined them again after a swift change of clothing. Certainly, their physical splendour needed some explanation. Inches over six feet, with heavy faces, heavy locks of hair—Zoe saw them as Greek warriors, or lovers, or athletes, on the frieze of some Ionian temple. Her esteem reached its peak when they were out on the field. Her eyes could never decide whether their running or their standing, poised to take a goal, thrilled her more.

Off the field, well, off the field, they still looked like heroes, but were as complex as a comic strip. Conventional. Ordinary. In spite of their looks. (She had just realised it.) They had the usual predatory view of Zoe, and no very strong hold on her affections. She had never thought of them so coldly as today, yet today she would willingly have gone to live with both of them at the same time.

With a sort of spite, she put her right hand in Tony's hand, and her left arm about Philip's waist. This was noticed. Laughing, the four young ones ran down the path to the gate beyond which stood two scarlet MGs.

Pausing to look back where the house and her family and those disagreeable orphans were invisible now behind the trees, Zoe felt a pang in her chest that made her sigh. Philip looked down. 'Out of breath,' she explained, smiling up at him.

•

Before either orphan reappeared at the Howards' house, Zoe had wrested the story of his meeting with them, and their life history, from Russell.

'Lie on the beach with me. Talk to me. In a few weeks I'll be so busy. There'll be a thousand people all over the house today. You'd only be collared and bored.' She said carefully, 'Your company means more to me than it does to anyone else,' then added for form's sake, 'Except Lily, I suppose.'

'*Yes.* Which I'd have said sooner, had that been humanly possible.'

They smiled.

'But pack us some lovely grub, Zo, and we needn't come back.'

So they lay on the beach. Since his return from the camp, after obligatory sessions with the doctors, Russell had eaten and exercised with a kind of purposeful dedication that no one could comment on. Zoe looked at her brother. He was slim, athletic, of medium height. At this early age, his brown hair was greying. He had his mother's pleasantly irregular features—high cheekbones, a slightly aquiline nose, and a large mouth with very white even teeth. His legs were scarred, and the scars on his back were visible as he stretched out on the sand in black swimming shorts. 'Ulcers,' he had said, once and for all. Zoe had learned to see these marks not only without appearing to, but really, without thinking or feeling.

She served out cold chicken and salad. 'But how did you meet the Quayles?' she demanded. 'Anna's nice, but he's so—weird.'

'No. What did he say to you?' Russell considered his plate with interest.

'It wasn't what he *said*…He asked if I'd done relativity.'

Russell opened his eyes at her, and she had to laugh, and scrutinise them as she often did. His eyes were luminous, a brilliant blue.

'Relativity! That could be his idea of small talk. Meeting just happened.'

Going by train to a suburb an hour out of town, visiting the wife of a friend who had died in the camp, he travelled in a carriage with someone who later turned out to be Stephen Quayle. A mysterious halt between stations prolonged itself to the point where his companion was forced to look up from his book. Russell was seen twisting his neck to read the title, because no line of print offering itself in that vacuum could go unread.

'Relativity?' Zoe bit without appetite at her chicken.

'That's not the *only* thing he's interested in. This was Catholicism, existentialism.'

'Is he one?'

'Not Stephen.'

Parting finally at the station, they had met again for dinner in town at night, and adjourned to Stephen's room near the city to continue the talk.

About to object, 'But you have so many friends. Why pick up this salesman for conversation?' Zoe stopped. None of this was true. Too many of his friends were dead. She should try to be pleased at this sign that he was willing to start again, she told herself.

'Has he been away?'

'He wasn't passed. Eyes.'

The two men had met three times before the Quayles visited Russell at home and met his family. Anna had been brought along because it happened to be a Saturday when Stephen was due to take her out: she still lived with the uncle and aunt who were her legal guardians, and Stephen saw her once a fortnight.

Their father had come to Australia from England to

negotiate a contract and to establish a new branch for the engineering company that employed him. He met a girl—Stephanie Boyd—at a dinner party in Sydney and married her a month later. When Stephen was seven or eight, and Anna a few months old, their parents were killed in a level-crossing accident.

'Their car hit by a train? They must have been so young,' Zoe argued in dismay, looking at Russell, wanting him to change his story.

He raised his shoulders and lowered them. He leaned across to the basket and threw some chicken bones into an empty container.

'Were the children in the car?'

'I think so. I don't know. I didn't ask for a diagram. You don't ask people to go into detail, Zo.'

She peeled a banana and ate a bite slowly. 'Were they nice—his mother and father?' She inspected his face. 'He showed you photographs of them. What were they like?'

Clambering up, rubbing his chest and shoulders free of sand, Russell said, 'You and Lily. You can both exercise second sight. You don't need me around. I'll just—have a swim, while you…'

'Ha ha!' But she had gone too far, tramped about, guessing so accurately. They knew each other well. He was going away, pounding down to the water, receding, receding, like a moving exercise in perspective.

You're good, she declared in her mind, as she looked stony-faced at the place where he had disappeared into the flat green water. Though she realised that that, like the scars and so much else, was not to be thought of, either. Rolling over, she picked herself up and ran down to the water.

Fifteen minutes later, they returned together to their basket, umbrella, books and sandals, shining, dripping, gasping for breath.

'Best swim for years,' Russell said, drying himself off, spreading his towel out and lying down again.

'You say that every time. I wish they'd put up a shark net. Finish off about your awful friend.' Zoe achieved a tone of exceeding neutrality.

Russell turned and looked at where she sat leaning forward over her outstretched legs appraising her knees as though they were valuable merchandise. She said, 'Go on. I'm all ears.'

'He's a funny cove. I like him. One of these days we might go into business together.'

'Business? What sort of business? You'd give everything away.'

'Wait and see.' He fixed his gaze on her. 'Do you want to hear more or not?'

'Please.' She sat meek and still, imitating a very good girl.

After the accident, the Quayle children were taken in by their mother's brother, a middle-aged solicitor, and his wife. Their father's brother, a London bachelor, wrote and sent money, and it was agreed that the children should stay where they were. But in spite of the contribution from England, they were in no way well provided for. The Quayles had lived to the limit of their income, in the knowledge of substantial prosperity to come. The company was an international one, and Quayle was highly regarded; anyone would have said his expectations were well-founded. He had laid no plans for something as unlikely as his own early death.

The uncle at Parramatta, Charles Boyd, was as concerned for his two wards as any childless man with a neurasthenic wife could be expected to be. He hoped the children would be an interest for Nicole, and improve her state of mind. She had been so shorn of tasks and responsibilities when it had occurred to him that social life was perhaps the cause of her many deep but indefinable troubles that her life was left utterly idle but no less beset by misery.

There was always some helper in the house—housekeeper, nurse—but none stayed long. It was to this chain of strangers that the children had to look for company and comfort. Their uncle was preoccupied with work and with his wife. Her melancholy and her moods had cowed him. He longed for peace, gave her her way, and had no peace.

Sometimes there would be an economy campaign: electricity would be saved, food and hot water and cleaning materials watched with a frenzied vigilance. Then there would be wild demented spending on clothes that were never worn; on clocks, rugs, cutlery, for a house already over-supplied with such items. Sometimes the children were bought hand-stitched garments, while necessities were not recognised as such by the hysterical and increasingly despotic Nicole. The rights and preferences of other adults, of two children who belonged to no one, vanished behind the doors of the handsome old brick house. Nicole was so very strange, if thwarted.

At first a nurse was hired to look after Anna. Then when she was old enough, she was sent to a nursery. Stephen went to a local school. He and his sister learned to be silent within miles of their aunt. They were obliged to think about her constantly, because it seemed that their survival depended on it.

Zoe said, 'Parramatta. That dull, dry, flat, hot place, *and* an aunt who's insane. Even I feel sorry for them.'

'Though he did ask you awkward questions?'

Impatiently, Zoe rattled her hands at him. 'What then? Anna's still there? Is it still the same?'

'So I gather.'

'And when did Stephen go? As soon as the legal age, I suppose. But why to this ghastly dead-end thing? If his uncle's a solicitor, couldn't he have arranged something better? He's probably good at everything.'

'He's bright enough,' Russell agreed. 'But there wasn't any money.'

Zoe looked as if she had never heard of it.

'Economics,' Russell continued. 'His uncle was no help. He's addled his wits by trying to think like *her* for years.'

'What? Is he mad, too?'

Eyeing her, Russell saw that she sounded more flippant than she was. 'He's wiped out. Exhausted. You can't humour someone out of a psychosis.'

Grabbing her dark wet hair fiercely in two hands, Zoe twisted it round, held the end on top of her head with her left hand while she searched for and found a tortoiseshell clip in her bag. She fixed it in place. 'I asked Stephen about scholarships, but he passed it off.'

'There weren't many even a few years ago. Different days. And nowhere to study.'

'But if the house was so quiet?'

Russell sat up. 'You must have got left over from the Spanish Inquisition. Throw me an apple.'

Silently, lids lowered, she leaned back on one elbow, took a red polished apple from the basket and handed it to him. She dusted dry sand from her arms and legs.

Looking at the apple before biting, Russell said, 'The two kids were quiet, but the house was earthquake country. Atmosphere turned on day and night. This aunt—Nicole—needs an audience. Keep in touch with Anna, Zo. She's...'

'Did he tell you all this?'

'Only a few things, and Anna's said nothing. But I've been out there. I've seen them together.'

Zoe pulled on a yellow cotton jacket, and her hair came down, and she fastened it up again. 'I can't make it all out. Do you think it's true? It sounds a bit...And a salesman! He must be doing it on purpose to amaze people.'

Over his apple, as she spoke, Russell seemed not only to watch her with those startlingly blue eyes, but to listen with them, too. He said, 'You don't know him. He'd never think anyone was interested enough to be amazed.'

To live without the interest or attention of other people, without making an impression: in her mind, Zoe groped to imagine such a state. All she could find was a feeling of irritation.

Russell said, 'He might do something yet. I've been working on him. Maybe one day people won't be wasted; talents won't be wasted. But when you think of that far-off time, you wonder how the not-wasted could ever flourish, with their fulfilment resting on so much'—he lightened his tone and finished off—'so much of what we've just been talking about—waste.'

Zoe looked at him dubiously, and dug her heels into the sand.

Under his breath, he said, 'All that innocent fertiliser.'

'But Russell…,' Inwardly, she had started to shake. Even her voice shook slightly.

'What? That isn't the way it is. There have always been individuals who've known how to use their lives. It always will be individuals who reach fulfilment. So that was a fairly rickety flight of fancy.'

'But Russell,' she said again. 'There's Stephen. Everything's just happened to him. But what about the men who've been little pit boys, down in the coal mines at thirteen, and then they work and turn into cabinet ministers.'

'What about them?' He started to pack methodically.

'Are we going? I'm trying to be serious.' She helped gather up the remains of the picnic, then plunged an arm into her beach bag for her mirror. What a very pretty face! What a lovely face, really! And still there!

Russell watched. 'But it's hard for you. Rising from pit boy to cabinet minister is a little more complex than going up in a lift.'

'Yes, sir! Yes, sir! I'll remember that, sir!' That glimpse of her own silken face had made her gay.

They smiled, and walked along the beach, then climbed the grassy verge to the roadway.

'We'll now go and mingle with our parents and that cheerful gang they're having a conference with. Educationists. What a word! Optimists.'

'Aren't you optimistic?' They started to trudge up the short hill as Zoe spoke.

'According to my lights. Not according to theirs.'

'How many weeks is it till the wedding?' Even to Zoe, her tone was unexpectedly sombre.

'Eight.' He bumped her arm to rally her spirits. 'We're not going away forever.'

•

Russell drove his friend's young sister into the country.

The company Stephen worked for had commanded him to appear in Melbourne; he would be away from Wednesday till Tuesday. Having heard the details of the trip, Russell volunteered to take Anna out, if this happened to be her Saturday, and Stephen made the arrangements with his uncle. Lily and Zoe were both busy, but wished the expedition well. Mr Howard gave up his car. Everything conspired.

It was a flawless, new-world morning, with every leaf

reflecting sunshine. The sky was boundless. Anna had stood by while Uncle Charles and Russell exchanged a few words, then they were through the streets, out and away. After a split-second of awe and awkwardness when she met him at the door, she was relaxed as a cat, but so full of life that she could have jumped out of her skin. Russell had only smiled into her eyes with the intense attention he gave to everyone. She had only smiled back with the same quality of attention. Among the glittering facets of the morning that they both noticed with surprise was this equal meeting of attention.

'We're going to see the best of everything today. Do you like the country? Tell me things, Anna Quayle.'

In the process of realising that she liked everything, that everything delighted her, Anna did as she was told. It was the beginning of the happiest day of her life.

She wore sandals and a pale yellow cotton dress. Her short fair hair curled naturally, trailing in fronds down the back of her neck, falling over her forehead, leaving her ears bare; her large golden hazel eyes were the colour of Stephen's eyes. Russell observed the details of her appearance with the surface of his mind; but as they continued to drive through miles of eucalypts, down into tropical valleys, up through rolling pastoral land, she seemed to fuse with the intense, direct and open light of the day, with the scent of the bush. They had both disappeared into the day.

A sun-dappled clearing overhung by tall trees drew the car to a stop. They crunched over the dry undergrowth of leaves and ferns, looking at the red and gold and white of wildflowers. Pale dust powdered Anna's toes. The silence was stupendous. There was a sense of branches and trunks leaning and listening.

They rested on a satiny silver-grey tree, long felled by age or storm. Lily had given Russell a pipe. Smoking had abandoned him in the camp, but Lily had given him this new pipe, so he tried again and again to light it. Anna laughed. He laid the stone-cold object in a bed of leaves and covered it. 'Lost. Our secret.'

While they leaned against the curves of this woodland chaise longue, Russell began to tell the girl about the camp. He thought she might be interested. It had never occurred to him to tell anyone else. He thought he had information that might be useful to her. He told her about his friends. One had been to Spain and there, between battles, had learned the local dances.

Tearing a sprig of pink blossom from a plant at his side, Russell clamped it between flashing teeth and gave a demonstration. It was the most vital physical action Anna had ever seen. 'Is that what Spain is like?'

Laughing, he flung himself down beside her again. 'An artiste needs a wooden floor.'

He told her about ingenuity, and the sharing of skills, about hope in a hopeless place. He told her about death and survival. They were silent for a while.

From a basket prepared by Mrs Howard, they took thermos flasks of tea, and home-made biscuits. They drove on through a landscape fragrant with fruit and flowers.

'I didn't know Australia was so beautiful!' Anna exclaimed, as though she were a foreigner, seeing it for the first time. She leaned out into the day, wind streaming over her. 'I thought it was dull.'

'That's the cunning part of our route. There's plenty of flat scrubby stuff around.'

At a coach house turned restaurant, they had lunch. After that, they drove to the edge of a river, one of the tributaries of the Hawkesbury. Anna paddled her feet to wash the dust off, then let them dry in the sun. They lay on the grass, watching birds and afternoon clouds. Afternoon. The afternoon came on.

They drove back towards Parramatta. Anna would have grieved to see the sun sliding down the sky, but for Russell's intention that she should not. The omissions in her story told him her life. Passionate, dispassionate, truthful, she might have been any age. What was it about the mingling of these qualities that made her so uniquely likeable, so agreeable to be with?

'We'll see you again soon,' he said, and they smiled, then he shook hands with Uncle Charles.

•

Mrs Howard led the friend known to the family as 'poor Ellen' through the house, explaining the manifold activities of workmen, caterers, acquaintances and relations.

'The house is hotching with people. I don't know who half of them are. It's the smallest possible wedding, Ellen.'

(This was apologetic, for poor Ellen had not been invited.) 'In a church, but not elaborate. Then a small gathering back here—her family and a few of their young friends, and then off they go.

'(Oh, the reception is here—I could see you thinking—because they have three rather elderly invalids at Lily's house. Rather frail. Wouldn't be fair. Her mother and father are really attending to all this.) And then a week later, they leave for London. Lily's going to work on her thesis, and Russell's finally agreed to buckle down, too. He's exercised in the local gym and practised swimming and diving and judo. He went off to the outback for a few weeks. He's devoured a couple of libraries, and played every record a hundred times. He also practises walking on his hands along the verandah. What he wouldn't do was think about a profession. Clive had I hoped he might opt for law and politics, but he's decided on political economy and later, social science. I can't quite see why. Luckily, he has that money from his grandfather, so they won't starve. We hate to lose him, but he must travel. If he and Lily hadn't had this—juvenile agreement, or if Lily had changed her mind while he was away, he'd have gone off as a free agent. Not that we wish it, of course!'

'Your voice can be heard all over the house.' Zoe came upstairs from her darkroom in the cellar.

'Did I say anything incriminating? I'm wound up. You take Ellen to my room for a moment while I see what those men are doing.' She dashed off.

Leading the way to her mother's small sitting room

upstairs, Zoe explained that a marquee had been erected in the garden but was now being dismantled because everyone quarrelled about it.

Ellen listened to the wedding talk. Thin, small, white-faced, with the bones showing through transparent skin, the possessor of a German husband named Hans, Ellen lived in a handsome house, made excellent crème caramel, and was once known to a younger Zoe as 'that sad lady'. The only words she ever seemed to utter to Mrs Howard in Zoe's hearing were, 'Hans and I can't go on like this, Alice.'

She was always so anguished, so convinced that a change of some quite fantastic nature was due to occur within the hour that, non-existent though Zoe's interest was in these adult matrimonial troubles, she was always jolted when she heard, months later, that nothing whatever had changed. It seemed uncanny that a grown-up woman could want and expect an event, and the event refuse her.

Just the last time Ellen was in the house, Zoe had said to her mother, 'What on earth *is* it?' But she only shook her head, saying, 'Ah, well...'

All that exhausted murmuring from her mother's room, as she dashed to the telephone, engulfed in her own affairs, struck Zoe as very feeble. 'Either Ellen should initiate some change and stop waiting for things to turn up, or put up with it better.'

Mrs Howard raised her eyebrows eloquently, saying nothing.

'Don't you agree?' Zoe insisted. 'Ah, you're such a

sympathetic friend.'

'And you're so the opposite.'

'Ah, well...Ah, well...' Mimicking her mother, she had rushed out of the room, away from miserable white faces and wasted years.

'I haven't seen you for weeks, Zoe. You're not a schoolgirl any more.'

'It's my hair. That changes every day.'

Mrs Howard arriving to rescue and replace her, heard this. 'No, Zoe's practically a student now. But we'll be keeping her at home with us for a few years, we hope.'

Rising from her mother's blue velvet chair, Zoe stood by politely before retreating, the object of attention even at this frantic time.

'Have you seen her photographs?' Mrs Howard asked. 'It's only a hobby. But she's spending more and more time on it. You knew she won that competition?'

Ellen made sounds of astonishment and respect, and watched Zoe with some avidity while her mother continued. 'Sometimes she takes one of her followers, and he stands about draped in paraphernalia while Zo has all the fun. She makes use of these young men.'

'No, I don't think so.' Zoe returned Ellen's scrutiny. 'I'm interested in what I'm doing, and they're interested in me. There's the doorbell. Excuse me.'

Well, the morning hadn't been wasted, she reflected, skimming downstairs. One, she had done some useful work; two, she had appalled Ellen by her vanity. She had discovered this high-handed, high-spirited manner of seeming tremendously well pleased with herself. No one took any notice but people like Stephen and poor Ellen, who reacted like nineteenth-century Church of Scotland clergy. Hell, devils, pitchforks, smoke and flames all laid on, and one immortal soul—hers—damned forever because she might appreciate herself above her true worth. Nice of them to be so concerned, she thought with some coldness. Having opened the front door in time to see one of the marquee men disappearing with another marquee man, she went back upstairs and changed her clothes.

Hunting through the house shortly afterwards for someone she could recognise, she came on her mother and Anna in the kitchen making coffee and sandwiches. Poor Ellen had gone. She and Anna greeted each other with enthusiasm and started to shout the day's news, laughing more or less continuously.

Mrs Howard said, 'You're incredible. Everybody keep quiet instead of egging everybody on. What was I going to say? Hand me those chives please, Anna. Stephen's gone down to warn the others they're not getting much for lunch. Where's Mrs Perkins, in the name of all that's holy? What do I pay her for? She should be doing this.'

'You sent her up the street to get some messages. She can't be everywhere.'

'Just don't develop a social conscience here and now, Zo. You've been without one long enough.'

All of the Howards except Russell claimed rather than

admitted to a bad temper, and regarded a certain fiery display as the sign of a lively and unrepressed personality. Zoe and her mother exchanged telling shots; Anna went out through the open door so quietly that no one noticed. Suddenly, Zoe sighed and stopped in mid-sentence, her interest in Mrs Perkins's rights, her mother's faults, evaporating totally. Staring into the nickel-plated surface of the percolator, she failed to see her own distorted reflection; to breathe in the delicious coffee scent puffing into the air.

On a ferry, coming home from town, she was questioning Russell.

'He's working, Zo. At night he writes out reports for his company and analyses sales. Then he reads.'

'He seems to live like a hermit, working and sleeping. Does he like women? Doesn't he like girls? You have just as much to do, getting everything cleared up to go away, but you see Lily.'

'Isn't she wonderful?'

'Yes. But what about Stephen? Doesn't he see any girls?'

'He doesn't see anyone much. During the day he has to talk sales talk hour after hour.'

'Someone like that!'

'That's why solitude's welcome. I don't think he knows many people. He isn't easy to know.'

'Is that natural? Is it natural?'

'What do you mean?'

'I don't know,' she said. 'I only wondered. To be satisfied. To accept it. Not to want to see people.'

Mrs Howard raised her voice. '*Zoe*. Turn off the percolator, and would you take this plate outside for me?'

Obediently, she glided out, glided back, glancing at her mother in abstraction. Mrs Howard saw this, and intending subtlety, began, 'I relented and made them a salad. Zoe...What did you think of the rehearsal last night? How did the orphan perform as best man?'

With a shiver, Zoe looked down. 'Don't call him that. That's so patronising. He stood about. I stood about. It doesn't take much of an IQ, after all.'

'Do you think Lily's reconciled?'

She shrugged indifferently. 'It's settled.'

'Well, I do think it's cantankerous of Russell to insist on having him. He's a stranger. Russell knows Lily's very attached to the family and all it stands for.'

'Family. That's just a word.'

Mrs Howard took a deep breath. 'Only because you've got one, Zo. Lily wanted that second cousin or whatever he is. And then she's landed with someone she hardly knows.'

'Russell *likes* him,' Zoe said, with quiet savagery. 'They can talk about things the second cousin couldn't even pronounce.'

Unconvinced, standing by the table ready to carry out her salad, Mrs Howard said, 'You know we'd have welcomed any of Russell's friends with open arms. Stephen could be a sort of foster son, but he makes it impossible.'

It was true. Zoe knew that Russell praised him constantly and defended him so that his family would not be affronted by Stephen's lack of grace, lack of warmth, by his erratic moodiness and prickliness.

Now, she asked excitedly, staring at her mother with sparkling eyes, 'But why all this? Why all this now? Why ask me? It's nothing to do with me. He isn't *my* friend.'

Mrs Howard studied the table carefully, picked up the salad bowl. 'No. But you never come out of that darkroom. You're invited out every night, and you won't go. You let Philip and Tony and the boys carry your gear about and then show them the door.'

'Why not? What's this? Trying to marry me off?' Zoe gave her mother a hostile look. 'They're too young.'

'And others are too old,' Mrs Howard commented.

Outside, there were footsteps and voices. Zoe picked up the platter of cheese and went out to join the group at the table. Over the pouring of coffee, her father and Lily were teasing each other. Talking, Mr Howard showed the perfect, strong white teeth that he had always taken so much interest in. His eyes were ingenuous. At least hundreds of people thought him very clever.

Russell was eating a sandwich and joking with a telegram boy who had come round to the side entrance and found his way into the party. Lily was helping to serve the salad. She turned, smiling, to give plates to Anna and Stephen, who were standing by the verandah wall, excluding themselves from the activity until they were made part of it. Moving cups forward for her father, Zoe covertly watched the others.

Lily was throwing off quips with such extraordinary rapidity that it was never possible to catch all she said. Now, as the plates were received, Zoe saw her give the Quayles a fixed stare of hauteur as her eyes met theirs. And Zoe realised that it was not only a sort of pity that Lily felt for anyone unrelated to her, but involuntary antagonism. Not much, almost invisible, but there. Lily resumed her story as though no vein of ice had been inserted in its midst: '—crashed headlong down the stairs knocking the vice-chancellor to the ground and came to rest on his substantial middle.'

'I'm being paid to remove her,' Russell said, walking over to them, finishing off his sandwich. 'Telegram. It says: Be happy.'

Coming up behind him, his mother confiscated it. 'You're not supposed to read them now.'

'Forget that message,' he said to Lily, and they both laughed, and Russell looked with delight at this tall girl with the tangle of rough blonde hair, the vital, angular face, at this strong girl whose voice had such thrilling qualities that her most ordinary utterance sounded significant.

With a shout of amusement, Mr Howard suddenly passed his open hand before Zoe's face. 'Woebegone! Russell's always been the great favourite with Zoe. She'd go to the dentist for him while we were still looking up the experts to see how to handle her. I don't think I've ever heard them exchange a cross word, and that's a pretty good record for someone with a temper like Zo's. What do you think?'

As visitors and the only people present who could be expected not to know these facts, Stephen and Anna, called on to respond, were momentarily silent. They had almost no idea how acquaintances in a group were supposed to talk to each other.

Anna said, 'We didn't see so much of each other.'

'Weren't you in the same house?' Lily asked, with that same slightly cold curiosity.

'Oh, yes. But—it was different.'

Mrs Howard interposed, 'No one can quarrel with Russell.'

'Not really a unanimous decision,' Russell assured his friends. 'I'd be inclined to say no one could quarrel with Anna.'

She smiled.

'That's the reason for the gloom,' Mr Howard concluded on a falling note. 'The last lunch.'

There were loud groans, a clattering of cutlery and a sudden discarding of plates.

With uneasy joviality, Mr Howard looked about at the rejected remnants. 'I've taken away their appetites,' he told his wife.

'They'll recover,' she said blandly. She had flower-like eyes, but was shrewd, and did value a light touch—something Clive singularly lacked. 'The telegram boy could have helped.'

'He was provided for,' Russell told her, and they looked affectionately at each other.

The telephone rang; the doorbell rang. Mrs Perkins answered one, Mrs Howard the other. There were new voices in the hall. Mr Howard went inside to go over some proofs, and shut himself in his work room with a faint air of having taken a vow of silence. Lily rose up from her chair and everyone looked at her, automatically comparing the colour of her skin with the colour of her hair.

'Like different shades of toast, you are, Lily,' Zoe told her. 'In Europe, you'll be pale.'

'What I'll be is ostracised, if I don't go home. My mother says I haven't taken enough part in the grisly discussions about something borrowed, something blue. No, I'll have to go. The house is full of aunts and uncles and grandparents and cousins who've winged their way over land and sea—'

'—for a last glimpse of our Lily.' Russell smiled at her.

'It *might* be a last glimpse. They're old, and we'll be gone for years.' She sounded genuinely regretful.

'I'll walk home with you.'

At once, Stephen turned to Anna. 'It's time we were off.'

'*Stay*. I'll be ten minutes. Keep them, Zo, or I'll blame you. We've got things to discuss, and this is the last chance.'

Zoe crossed her arms firmly to control the inner shaking that set up in her whenever she was face to face with Stephen. They had not exchanged a word this morning, which was not to say that they had been unaware of each other. It was one of many long expressionless glances that her father had intercepted and with his usual aplomb misinterpreted a short time earlier. If their eyes had nothing agreeable to convey, only some sort of resistance and resentment, they nevertheless had the greatest trouble in parting. And when they looked elsewhere that, too, was difficult. Because, somehow, he must know her well to disapprove of her so. His criticism mattered dreadfully.

Russell brought home from his meetings with Stephen an

air of having spent his time with someone valuable. Giving a harsh opinion for the pleasure of having it contradicted, she would demand, 'Where's his initiative? Why is he so lethargic?'

'Zo,' was all he answered.

But that was no answer. Stephen. Perhaps Russell saw him as a fellow prisoner? Everything about him was puzzling. She wanted to assure him of so much, although what he so urgently needed to hear, she could not always remember. There were times when she would have picked up any unknown man of any age from any park, and vowed to do this very thing at the next convenient moment. This, however, did not seem to be that same straightforward urge.

She said, 'You must stay, or I'll be in strife. Russell wants to discuss...Are *you* going away? Are you going overseas, too?' This possibility turned certainty as she spoke, simultaneously flashing from her eyes to his, and sending new shock waves through her body.

'No. Why?' For once, Stephen seemed interested.

She withdrew hastily. 'I just wondered—what there could be to discuss when he'll be away.' Left with her half-question, she looked at him in despair. Something in him took her from the pink marshmallow castle of her life to a high cliff over the ocean in the real world. Before this, only Russell was real. Now, Stephen pretended not to know, was scarcely even civil. In a moment, with one word, she could give him—what he had always wanted. Himself. Happiness. She thought. Perhaps. Something. A vital message.

Through black eyelashes meshed against the sun, through

his spectacles, he stared at her.

'You could read the paper, if you haven't seen it.' Zoe jumped up. 'I want to show Anna something in my room.'

Without comment he lifted the paper by his chair, beginning to open the wide pages. Zoe walked away. Everything they said was true. You could feel physically torn from someone you weren't even touching.

'Leaving Stephen to himself?' Mrs Howard asked, as they went towards the stairs. 'Oh, you're taking Anna up.' Because this had been prearranged. She had said, earlier in the day, 'Why not give Anna some of those dresses you never wear?'

Zoe was doubtful. 'Could you offer her second-hand clothes?'

'Why not? She'd be grateful, if she has any sense.'

'It looks like charity. *I* wouldn't like it.'

'She's only a child.' If anything irritated Mrs Howard it was this sort of shrinking sensibility: there were, after all, larger issues at stake everywhere. 'Just as you please, darling, but you'd be doing her a kindness.'

A kindness! With a sort of jaundiced shudder, Zoe turned away. On the one hand, the voice of her mother's experience, which naturally could not be very extensive; on the other, her own instinct. And what a lot of it she had!

Now, however, having left Stephen downstairs, she could think of nothing else. He despised her. An invisible hand dragged a steel rake through her body. Zoe threw herself on her bed, turning her head restlessly and breathing with a physical distress that was almost inconceivable to her. 'Oh, Anna!

Oh, Anna! It's so hot. Or is it cold?' She gave a fretful laugh and sat up to study Stephen's sister.

His lion-coloured eyes. Her rounded chin. She was like a Roman girl, the statue of a Roman girl in the days of Imperial Rome. Sometimes, rather a plain one, if the aunt and uncle had been awful; at other times, there was something very pleasing to see. Her appearance reflected her feelings, her state of mind, as though what she contained was stronger than her flesh. On the plain days, Zoe occasionally wished she would go home. I am very sensitive to faces, she told herself. A visual person. That her own prepossessing exterior mirrored rather exactly her rare and beautiful self, she had never doubted.

'Anna...Does Stephen mind about being best man? (Do sit down.) I mean, all the fuss. What does he say?' she asked lamely.

'Nothing. But I suppose he knows why Russell asked him.'

'Why did he?' Zoe was intent, leaning nervously forward.

'Well. Because he wanted us to be official. He wanted us all to know each other when he's gone. Didn't he?' To see Zoe engrossed, dependent on her opinion, evidently caused Anna doubts.

'Did he say so?'

'No-o.' Anna spoke on two equivocal notes, and stared at the irregular pattern on the rug that covered part of the polished wooden floor. Without real attention, she eyed the photographs pinned on a panel of the wall facing the windows, the tiny hand-painted Mexican figures, the three glass snowstorms, records, the turquoise and green balloons, the typewriter on the desk, the many books stacked into shelves in the wall. Outside, there were leaves, clouds, blue space.

A broken fingernail. Zoe stared at her hands with displeasure. Then, quite having lost touch with that instinct she had intended to follow, she suddenly jumped from the bed and, sliding back the door of her wardrobe, dragged out a number of dresses.

Up off the chair, Anna shot, her eyes growing larger by the second. She backed away, saying, 'I don't need anything.'

As if she had unwittingly fired a revolver point blank at someone she had never seen before, Zoe's own eyes and face opened with a sort of belated, reciprocal shock. 'I know you don't *need* anything. You'd be doing me a favour. One of my ratty ideas. Stay here while I get us some coffee. We both missed out in all the turmoil down there.'

Escaped, dropping from stair to stair, she gave a series of low groans, not having to imagine self-indulgently what it might be like to be Anna. This small blow was *in addition to* the rest of her life. Suffering, endurance, were things Zoe herself knew nothing about, except through art, and because of Russell. And even that, what she had seen and read that pushed beyond her own experience, had the very muted impact, she realised now, of watching an experiment in chemistry, never having studied the subject.

In the kitchen, she waited for the coffee while Mrs Perkins, washing dishes, talked about illness.

And Stephen, too. Those looks he gave as if from another country; perhaps they were justified. After all, she thought, the orphans and Russell are like each other, different from me. She pondered while the coffee heated and Mrs Perkins maundered on about hearts and livers. Even Russell was fatiguing, she thought with self-pity. How careful you had to be with people like that! Her mother was right. She had no time for melancholy egoists, shrinking violets. The golden mean. Nothing too much. Moderation in all things, her mother said. Nervous breakdowns, her mother said. I could have a nervous breakdown any day I liked. But she did *not* like. She was too strong to consider falling over when life was strenuous.

'Coffee boiled is coffee spoiled,' Mrs Perkins said.

'We won't mind.' Zoe assembled mugs, sugar and milk, and took four cream cakes as an afterthought.

Or *would* Anna mind? How could she tell? Zoe started back upstairs, avoiding what sounded like a scene from *Macbeth* in the sitting room. The idea that she might have to proceed through life without ever knowing what anyone would mind and, if she decided to care, having to take quite supernatural precautions not to cause any damage, appalled her.

She remembered a party given for some of her father's students. A supposedly quick-witted girl called Ruth had contributed an anecdote about someone hailing her at the Quay, calling 'Ruth' in the middle of the afternoon so that everybody heard. Responding to Zoe's blank gaze, the girl only repeated, still irate at the memory, '—called my name and everybody looked.'

Like a primitive, Zoe had thought. Stone-age men guarded their names like that. How could mere forethought warn anyone that a frothy blonde girl of nineteen felt the same?

Balancing the tray on her raised thigh, Zoe opened the door. Anna sat in one of the deep corduroy chairs, holding a balloon lightly on her lap. Her face expected nothing good. Inwardly, Zoe reeled with dismay. Had *she* done this? To *his* sister?

'Could you move those big books off the table? Now let's ruin our statistics with these cakes.'

Looking forward across her eyebrows as she leaned over the table, she glanced apprehensively at Anna, who stood turning the pages of a book she had shifted to the desk. Zoe recognised a flash of colour as a page fell, and started to talk about the painting. Standing together with mugs and cakes, flipping through a history of western art, the girls were stilted.

In her mind, Zoe felt the pressure of Russell and Stephen and Anna in her life, and their peculiar demands—and worse, the limit of their demands. She was too young to be thoughtful, or interested in someone else's problems. She felt a huge impatience at this unwarranted check to her self-absorption and happy conceit and ambition. So they had all had more troubles than she. Did that really make them superior? If two men were walking along the street and a brick fell on one, missing the other, did that make the injured one a better person? All he had learned was what it was like to have a brick fall on his head. It had happened to him. Why make a virtue of it?

It was not as though she were a trashy or frivolous person. Or not *only* trashy and frivolous. She was almost certain her heart was in the right place. It was simply that circumstances had not called on her to produce it very often. If Stephen drifted away when Russell left for Europe, if he could be as boorish and uninterested as that, Zoe had half-supposed till this moment that she would let Anna drift off, too. Why not? She had enough friends. It was awkward to know people who had less money and no proper home.

Depressed, she swallowed the last of her cake. Like a speeded-up film, she ran through her mind the picture of Anna's life—school, the creepy aunt falling into hallucinations and delusions, the extinguished uncle, the inhuman Stephen. Subtract *us*, Zoe thought, and that's what's left. This was what they meant by wrestling with your conscience. She said, 'Promise you'll come over when Russell's gone. You and Stephen. We'll ask you, and you'll come, won't you? Otherwise, we'll think you only wanted to see Russell.'

Anna was evasive. 'Stephen's been transferred to Melbourne.'

As though a searchlight had flooded her, and then been switched off, Zoe said, 'Oh…No one told me. Let's join the throng downstairs. Hysteria seems to be setting in, from the sound of things.'

•

Mrs Howard switched on the lights and opened the french windows: several moths shot past her into the room like bargain hunters after prey. She flapped at them.

'No, but you're so personal, Zo.' There were times when her children daunted her. Her husband had churchmen, farmers, craftsmen, minor artists, a few black-sheep labourers in his background. Fortunately, there had always been some money. *Her* side was blameless: academics, solicitors, reliable men and women of one sort and another, all getting on with the business of the world. Yet somehow out of this mixter-maxter she was landed with strange offspring. Russell went beyond her and Zoe was not like her in a way she would have resented greatly had not they and all their attributes in a sense belonged to her.

'Yes, you're too personal,' she repeated to Zoe.

'What should I be? Mechanical?'

'Personal relations are not all there is to life, Zo. That's sloppy thinking. I have a full life, husband, children, but where I would be without work as well, I don't know. You're too intense lately about your likes and dislikes. So extreme about everything. You'll come to grief, if you invest your life in individuals. I've seen it happen.' She felt in the pocket of her dress, then cast an eye anxiously over the room's surfaces in search of the last of a hundred lists concerning the wedding.

'Well, you can't want me to invest it in worms and flies the way you do. And if this is what I'm like…'

'There's no need to pretend to be more ignorant than you are. This might only be a phase. Heaven knows, we've had a few.'

'How do you recognise one?' Zoe tore the wrapping from some things she had bought earlier in the day—a black

48

cashmere sweater, a silk scarf.

'By its passing. And by its excesses while present. Have you seen my list, Zo?'

'No. Where did you have it last? But mightn't it be that the way you look at things is a phase that hasn't ended? Isn't this a delicious red?' She held up the scarf.

'Lovely. But there are moments, when I'm talking to you and Russell, when I wish I'd never married. Go to bed now and take that reading list and some books with you. Your history's very shaky.'

'Go to bed! In Africa, I'd be a grandmother by now!' Still, it was infantile to be so irritating, and she had many choices and could choose not to be. Smiling with a sort of reciprocal indulgence, she and her mother embraced.

Not infantile at all, she thought about Stephen and went upstairs.

•

'How many came to this…?' Stephen indicated the illuminated garden, the house lit up like an ocean liner.

Russell and Lily had driven off. By a resurgence of the luck that had only recently deserted her, not by design at all, Zoe and Stephen were the last to saunter back down the path from the waving and kissing. It was a mild, glamorous night with stars but no moon.

'Scores. Hundreds. I don't know.' Zoe kicked her long dress out in front as they slowly walked. 'I didn't know you were going to Melbourne,' she said, in a strained voice. 'Anna told me a couple of days ago. When do you leave?'

'On Tuesday.'

'Almost at once! They didn't give you much time.'

'Just a few weeks.'

'I see. You didn't mention it.'

'I told Russell.'

They avoided the house and meandered down a path between high rhododendrons, both looking at the ground.

'Did you have any say in it? Did you have to go?' Zoe asked.

'I could have resigned. But companies don't like you to refuse promotion.'

'I thought popularity'—Zoe twisted off a leaf and dropped it—'was the last thing that bothered you.'

Just then she half-thought she heard a voice in the distance call, 'Help!' Occasionally, at night, it seemed to her she heard someone far off call out, 'Help!'

'The salary increase won't keep anyone in luxury, but Anna won't have to go without school books.'

He was so familiar to her that she was tempted to say, 'Spare me! Why the lies?' Because school books! Who lived today in a world where supplying one girl with school equipment was any sort of problem? He ought to think up a more convincing story. Who wanted for anything? (Except pensioners, she added scrupulously. Having seen old people shopping for food, having watched surreptitiously the careful examination of small coins, she was included to believe *they* might want.) But for Stephen to tell this weak story!

'I thought Anna was your *uncle's* problem.' At her side, she heard a deep breath.

Out of the darkness, Stephen said, 'He's had an invalid wife for years. Doctors and hospitals cost money. Nurses. All the rest of it.'

Zoe's mind was arctic, her attention so fine, that she understood everything.

Casually, brushing her hand now against her long skirt, now against the hedge of leaves on her right, she said, 'Down the hill at Lily's place they have three sick people. That's why the reception was held here, tonight. But they manage to scrape along in reasonable comfort.' She had the impression that this was not exactly what she had intended to say.

Their shoes sounded on the flagged path. Zoe's words repeated themselves in the living silence between them. She had a feeling that neither of them had chosen to speak the words that had emerged. It was as if two angular creatures made of metal and wire, invisible, standing outside, above and all round them, had spoken instead, mistranslating with malice. She felt helpless, and through the hardness of heart and the sense of grievance put on her by the invisible controller, she could feel Stephen's helplessness.

He said, 'I think I'll look for Anna. It's time I took her home.'

'Do we see you again?'

'Annual holidays.' He said, 'I don't suppose you would ever be in Melbourne?'

'I don't suppose I would.'

Inflexibly held by their robot masters, they were guided down the path and into the house and Stephen found Anna and said good night and goodbye.

Mrs Howard put an arm round Zoe's waist and drew her into a circle of laughing, middle-aged faces. She knew them all. They gave her the customary hungry detailed looks. Everyone had drunk and eaten well. They appeared genial and satisfied. Zoe smiled and said their names, responded to their questions under the guidance of the automatic control. Dr Hope prescribed another glass of champagne. She drank it down. Her mother said in an aside, 'Is something wrong?'

Her light eyes, with their curious silvery glaze, turned to the familiar face. 'What?'

'You're rather—'

'What?'

'Sharp. A little.'

'What did I say?' Zoe's voice was like a voice in a dream.

'You won't keep this one long, Alice.'

Eyes: two, four, six, eight, ten, twelve eyes. All knowing what they knew. Mrs Howard glanced amusedly across her shoulder at Zoe, who could be teased and sometimes had been.

And, 'Biologists!' she would say then, while her mother smiled. 'You're so scientific and enlightened. You make me think of animals. (I don't mean *you* remind me of animals.) But animals copulating. Like a butcher's shop.'

'And you're not an animal, Zoe?'

Then she would always pause, her eyes unfocussed. 'No, I don't think so. Not exactly. Not entirely.'

But tonight she only smiled in a way that was inexplicably different from the shining, eager-eyed smiles of other days and, while the watchers let themselves be stirred, murmured something about her friends and moved off.

'She's quite a girl, Alice. Makes me feel my age to see her so sophisticated.'

'That's mostly an act. Oh, she's too much of a good thing,' her mother said, depreciating her treasure. 'But still very young.'

'Hullo.' Noiselessly, she approached Philip, who appeared to be moping about by himself at the dark end of the verandah. 'Are you moping, or do I only think you're moping?'

He turned from a prolonged staring into the garden behind the house. Taller than Stephen. Black hair, very level black brows and very level eyes like aquamarines.

'You have what they call a striking glance,' Zoe told him, knowing how he had been made to wince for his beauty. He was cheered on during his victorious runs on the football field by a variety of ardent nicknames. 'Literally, you could make people fall right over, looking at them like that.'

'Not you.'

Silent, they leaned together out into the night over the broad stone wall of the verandah.

'Why not me? Let's go somewhere.' Zoe was gazing down at the shadowed lawn.

'Anywhere?' Slowly, mistrustfully, Philip came to life,

staring at the side of her head.

'Anywhere. You go up to the car. I'll get out of this drapery and be with you. Fifty seconds.'

At the gate five minutes later, with a scarf on her dark hair, breathing the clammy breath of the Pacific and a million flowers and trees, with her hand on the wide painted top of the gate, she paused before sliding back the bolt and lowered her head. She lowered her head instinctively, and thought: that is that.

•

Anna wrote in her journal: *I have been on my own for a week now.*

It was like having been dragged bleeding profusely, dangerously wounded, but alive, from the battlefield. She could not smile enough, marvel enough, at the words. She wrote another word, a fantastic understatement.

It is a great relief. Everything smells dusty, and the carpet has a hole that keeps tripping me. But I'm free. At first, I could smell the gas stove, which is next to the bed, but the window is always open. Other people have rooms here, but you never see them. You hear them throwing the furniture about, and running water, and know when they are cooking.

Mrs Howard told Uncle Charles that this was a respectable place, with no wild people. An old lady she knew stayed here once. Uncle Charles thinks I am mean, going away to live. He said I could go in by train to the office every day from Parramatta. *Her* idea. He only has *her* ideas.

Mrs Howard thought I should keep on with Charles and Nicole to cheer them up. She said I exaggerated. She warned me that I would be much worse off, trying to keep myself on a junior clerk's wage. You can't explain anything to a rich, lucky person. They don't know. They talk about 'cases' and people who have 'problems'. They read a lot about them, but don't know. Mrs Howard asked me why I was so ungrateful. I tried to tell her that they pressed lies on me every day, and tried to make me agree the lies were true, looking me in the eye. Charles's soft voice. It felt as if they wanted to murder me.

I can see it looks a bit dramatic. But if anyone sane had ever listened, they would not have disagreed with me. Mrs Howard opened her eyes very wide and pretended to be shocked. She said, 'Dear, dear! Hidden fires!' She was quite jeering. I felt all wrong, even though I am aware of so much, really.

Anna chewed at the end of her pen and sighed, feeling the existence of some law that made all such claims ridiculous. And yet, she insisted to herself, I do know something they don't.

It was not that the Howards called black white, like Charles and Nicole. They knew what was what. They gave little lectures all the time, and since they were lecturers, this did not impress Anna as unnatural. At their house, she had listened to talks on youth, wine, education, painting, the Liberal Party, the Labor Party, birth control, the First World War, the Second World War, the Third World War, fashion, newspapers, society, travel, opera, theatre, music, cooking, sculpture, the Art Gallery, town planning, universities, traffic, mental illness, Aborigines, foreign countries, restaurants, dancing and sailing.

In fact, there was no particular topic she could recall not having been lectured on by Zoe's parents. And yet there *was* one, even if she could not remember what it was. And it was this subject that mysteriously mattered more than all the others together.

Anna wrote:

Mrs Howard asked me for an example of what I meant when it was everything. I told her that because Nicole was ill, she had always to be right. We were supposed to be like Polonius, changing course to agree with Hamlet, no matter what. And since Charles had decided that Nicole had to be right, someone had to be wrong.

Mrs Howard said, 'You're young and healthy. You can stand it.'

I said, 'Not every day. She would accuse me of anything that came into her head. However bad it was, Charles always pretended to believe her, or did believe her, which means he is ill now, too.'

This made Mrs Howard quite angry. She said you

shouldn't take things personally when people were ill, and that the things I'd told her were puerile, or petty, or something.

I said nothing. People ask to hear unpleasant things from curiosity, then feel outraged when they do. Besides, perhaps the things I told her did sound puerile. Perhaps they were the wrong incidents. There were so many.

It was like expecting three grains of sand to illustrate a ten-mile beach. But even multiplied they might have sounded nothing. Anna only knew that what they intended, and what she felt, were strong as life and death.

'Nobody likes self-pity, Anna,' Mrs Howard said.

'Not everyone has equal reason to feel it, Mrs Howard. Some things are sad, even if they happen to you yourself. But self-pity would mean I'd have to think about them, and I never do.'

Again, Anna stopped writing. It was easy to say that. But already, at this age, she had used more energy merely staying alive and holding on to herself in the tornado than Mrs Howard had yet had to call on in her fifty or whatever years. Now, like someone released from prison by the miraculous intervention of unknown friends, with spikes, clamps, thorns and a suit of nettles removed, she felt tired to the soul. She could have slept for a long time, into another life.

Anna continued:

Then Zoe came home and Mrs Howard went in to
another room and came back with an eggbeater for me.
She is kind, but has strict ideas about what ought to be.

It was a fact, and Anna admitted it to herself, that she would
not have liked *Russell* ever to hear a word of complaint fall from
her. But then she had not, strictly speaking, complained to Mrs
Howard. She had simply answered questions truthfully. There
was no way of making that truth jolly. And then, as for Russell,
he knew all that mattered by looking at you and talking about
other things.

She wrote:

One thing I'll remember about the Howards forever—
walking into the house one summer evening with
Russell and Stephen. Out in the laundry, we found
Russell's mother and father home from work, each with
a whisky glass in one hand and a piece of the family
washing in the other. Mrs Perkins was ill, so they set to,
to sort the washing out and get it into the machine.

They were talking and laughing about something
at work, not concentrating on the washing a bit. In a
little while, it was all hung out. More like a festival than
hard labour. I had no idea that dull jobs could be done
like that. I loved them for it.

She had thought their good nature almost supernatural. In memory, the laundry lights shone down on the Howards' heads like light from another world.

Zoe came in on her way home last night. She thought the room was small, but convenient. Next year, when she graduates, she is going to Paris. I told her I had read in a paper at work that she has a brilliant future. Zoe laughed. 'How would they know?' she said. She has told me before about two different opportunities. One is with a man who takes still photographs, a Frenchman; the other is with a film man whose headquarters are in Paris. They have seen her work, or heard of her somehow. She will be an assistant. One of them is famous. What I still can't understand is how they all knew about each other in the first place. Paris is so far away, and so many people must want these jobs. Zoe said they know about each other through friends. 'Everyone seems to be your family's friend.'

When I said this once before, years ago, to Zoe, she looked taken aback. 'But it's the same for you,' she said. 'We all know each other. The world really is quite a small place.'

'Oh, no. Most of us don't know anyone.'

Anna could still remember the way they batted startled looks to and fro.

Stephen says, 'These women, Zoe and her mother, they have a brutal confidence. Steer clear of them. They'd trample you to death. You're not as tough as they are. Don't think they're like Russell because they're related to him.'

Anna gloomed at the paper, recalling how she had reproached him. She had felt abused by these harsh words about her friends. After uttering cries of outrage, she argued with Stephen closely, following him about like a duellist in some Hollywood film of cardboard palaces.

'Zo's mother is older, and she *is* confident because of knowing more about biology than other people. She gives us lessons in a way, but I like it. People of my age bore me. They don't know anything. She's used to moulding students. I'm not very malleable. But all Zo is is happy.'

'Is she?' he asked, with a sudden, moody interest. 'Why should she be happy?'

Speechless, Anna turned his judgments over in her mind. 'Why?' she repeated, limp with astonishment. 'I *like* to see someone happy. The Howards are the first happy people I've ever known. They're wonderful.' How could she explain clearly enough to him? Why could he not feel it, too?

'You're a generous girl,' her brother said.

'No,' she said, exasperated. 'They're generous. They've been good to me.'

Stephen gave an angry, bitter exclamation. 'Grateful and adoring. Just what they want you to be.'

'I'm not! I'm not! You couldn't be more wrong.'

'Don't you see what a lift you give them? How would they know they were lucky if they didn't have someone like you to patronise? People like you provide the necessary contrast.'

'I'm not *people*,' she cried, indignantly. 'And far from humble. The very opposite. I don't think they're *better* than I am.' She gave him a look of furious pride and self-respect, then said, very slowly, spreading the syllables out, 'But—I—a–pprec–i–ate—them.'

'Oh, well. In that case. What are we arguing about? I can stop worrying.'

'Please do.' After a second, in an entirely different tone, she asked, 'Do you worry?'

'Not as much as I should,' he told her, with compunction.

'I didn't know.'

'The things you don't know.'

'And yet,' she said, 'I think all the time.'

One of the invisible tenants was frying fatty bacon. Anna shuddered and stopped breathing, a useful knack she had acquired.

Looking at the last words she had written: *Don't think they're like Russell because they're related to him*, she added hastily, ritually, *This is not the whole truth.*

•

Anna sat down at the table facing the window. Across the street, through the curtains, she could see as though in a looking-glass, ravaged two- and three-storeyed houses identical with those on this side of the street. Once grand, their situation was by this time their sole asset. Behind Anna, in rooms at the front of the house, was the harbour.

Jim at the office, a married man, one of the salesmen, every day brought her yesterday's newspaper, and yesterday's paper said Sydney Harbour was the most beautiful in the world. Some experts talked about the Greek light; others thought the whole country more like Spain; others again thought Sydney was the Paris of the Pacific. It was a far cry from droughty Parramatta, the harbour. It was the chief thing about Sydney to admire, but everywhere, it seemed to Anna, there was a wistful longing to be impressed and a lack of impressive sights. She didn't know what was missing.

For a view of a sailing ship from overseas, or some fireworks, or destroyers, crowds that never thought of ships or fireworks waited hour after hour on the harbour's edge. Afterwards, though these semi-spectacular events in the city's calendar never turned out as heartening and thrilling as hoped, the waiters told each other *they had been there*. Any advertised cause for joining a throng had hordes assembling. The reason mattered hardly at all.

And yet, on certain days, when mist and clouds and light combined ideally, from the harbour the city did have a look of cloud-capped towers. Unsubstantial. A beautiful mirage. And the sky was incomparable.

'When you're a child, the size of the continent on the map makes you proud of the place,' Mr Howard said. 'The space and the freedom to move about have a good effect on a young mind. But when you're older, it's a deprivation not to be in Europe. Your links with the human race are there.'

His listeners, Zoe and Anna, gave each other a look, inclined to giggle.

'That's just snobbishness,' his daughter said. Then, 'Think of what they've done in Europe! Why do you stay, then?'

'Because, if you've had that childhood I mentioned, you're an outrider, willy-nilly. But, historically, we're so thin on the ground here that the life would be meagre if you didn't put up a struggle.'

Zoe laughed. 'What are *you* struggling with?'

'What's it look like? My fishing tackle for tomorrow.'

'Oh, that's right. You're going miles out, aren't you? Is it a big boat?' She kissed his cheek, with her eyes open.

He smiled. 'Big enough. And as for Anna's wistful parade joiners, that's what they're trying to do, if they know it or not. Improve the content of their lives. And that's why others stay away.'

'If you hadn't been there,' Zoe said later to her young friend, 'he'd have blamed it all on a shortage of sex. He gets all pompous and didactic when you're around.'

'Do you think he's right about over there?'

'What? About everything being better?' She leaned down and dangled her fingers at Marmalade the cat, who patted her with a snowy paw. 'No. And he'd throttle anyone else who said it. For some people, his "content of life" must be better than it could be for the same sort of person here. It depends on what you're like. *Who* in particular, not where, is what matters to me. My company. My mother says that's unlucky. I don't know why.'

•

In the diary, Anna wrote:

> A card came from Russell today. He often goes to
> Italy during those long vacations they have at universi-
> ties. He and his friends work for some civilian relief
> organisation, and Lily stays in London, concentrating
> on her career.
>
> Stephen is sarcastic about Russell sending me
> cards and letters. He says Russell enjoys his own
> kindness. My brother does damp things down, even
> though Russell is his best friend. Only because he's
> afraid to trust anyone much.
>
> I wonder if he does think he's kind, writing? I
> wonder if it could be wrong to want to please someone?

After a pause, Anna answered herself: *Yes, it could be wrong, if you were not willing to let that person please you equally.*

'Next question,' she muttered to herself, choosing to pass over the problem of Russell's kindness and what it meant.

The population of her world was tiny, her experience extreme but limited. Even so, Stephen had no need to warn her, as though she lived in a pretty dream, that things were not always what they seemed. But still. One thing was plain as day, and Stephen did not deny the first part of the proposition—that some people intend their fellows harm. The other half was what he objected to—that some people are perfect. Willing though he was to agree to the darkness of life, he would not allow her the light. And he was wrong. The Howards were perfect. Of course, even among perfect people, some are more perfect than others.

She wrote herself several news items.

Zoe says what am I going to do with my life. Must think.

In England, they meet Lily's two sisters now and then. One is at Oxford. The other one is teaching at a university in Manchester. They are both older than Lily. The Manchester sister is married. They all sound very clever.

•

Jim Brady at work asked me a few days ago how much I was paid. When I told him, he stood quite still. 'Is that the ordinary rate?'

'For a girl of my age.'

'I suppose you live with your mother?'

'No. By myself.'

He had been eating a sausage roll (it was lunch time), but he stopped quite still again with his teeth sunk in the pastry, and thought. Then he took his teeth out of the pastry. 'How do you manage then, love?'

When I said I managed very well, he looked relieved. Today, he brought me three oranges from a tree in his backyard. I hope no one minded. He has some little children. And a wife, of course. He is cheerful, so I like him. I hear his stamp, stamp, stamping along the corridor every morning, with his shoes all shined and his toes turned out, and his face and hair polished. He has only worked for this company for a few weeks, but he is so enthusiastic you would think they had made him managing director. Great opportunities for the right man, he says. I don't know. I'd hate him to be disappointed. He is so positive. He is straightforward like a man in an old-fashioned advertisement. He seems to be listening to something that happened a long time ago, when he would have been more at home.

The other man in the office is Tom Crane. Tom is thirty and is married and has some little children, too. We are all new together. This is like Stephen's company, with the main office in Melbourne. They have just opened this branch. They sell office equipment. All over the state, all over Australia, thousands and thousands of men are driving into the country selling things—shoes, soft drinks. Tom's excited about his job, too, but he and Jim are different from each other and pretend when they meet, and put on important looks, like native chiefs trying to petrify each other. Tom is handsome and full of high spirits, but worries about supporting his family. This is what Jim worries about, and maybe this is why they are secretive and competitive. They both need to seem best to head office. For a couple of days they're friendly, then yesterday they tried to squash each other's bright ideas, jumping on words as if they were demolishing buildings.

Have soaked washing. Must hang out under house now. Will then read. Go to City Library every second day more or less for books. Would like wireless. Must make list.

•

Zoe came in with Russell's latest letter. Lily is having a baby. They are very happy.

•

Yesterday I went into the Botanic Gardens to lie down on the grass. Here, there is nowhere except your room. In the gardens you see other people alone. You have to walk miles to find flowers, so I looked at trees instead, reading their labels. After that I lay down in the middle of acres of grass. It smelled warm. When you are young, you are supposed never to be tired. Mr and Mrs Howard and all their friends go so fast.

'Imagine sleeping away your weekends!' they said.

'I like to lie down in the open air. I don't go
to sleep.'

'Is it the office that's troubling you?'

Anna had laughed. After three weeks in the office, she had
known that no emergency was beyond her. The days were busy,
but as though she were playing a game in the course of which
it was essential to make a move every two seconds. The ease of
it delighted her. Just how long she would be able to feel pleasure in a process so undemanding, she had not asked herself.
That the game was far different for the two men, she could see:
they had to brace themselves every day to go into the line of
fire, at the mercy of others.

Still, it was a fact that she tired easily, and had no choice
but to lie in the sun when she could. She lay with her face
down, her forehead and cheeks and bare arms pricked by the
short mown grass. She breathed the fresh earth odours and
they fed her. She lay so heavily relaxed and weary that she
seemed to sink and grow into the comfortable ground. And as
though it were a person, she began to feel fond of the country,
from being so close to it.

The Howards looked at Anna, taking a rapid interest
before leaving for a theatre, and Anna looked back as though
she were a china ornament. As they strolled past the windows
on their way to the car, Mr Howard said, 'She's a strange child.
Probably only suffering from adolescence.'

Inside the house, selecting records, Zoe and Anna
overheard and exchanged looks.

Anna continued to write.

Foreign men keep talking to you in the gardens. Dark foreign men most often, but some fair ones, too. They are all migrants, very polite and lonely. They practise their English. The main thing about them is loneliness.

Always willing to listen and talk, Anna also always went away. She would not waste anyone's small deposit of hope.

Keep imagining have lost money out of bag. Have decided to write down what get and what spend. Tom gave me old account book. I told Jim girls managed, but don't know how unless they earn more than I do. Stephen said would help with rent till income improves. Otherwise, would have had to stay with Charles and Nicole. How do girls manage? How do companies think girls manage? Next question.

•

Letter from Stephen. Hopes I am well. This science course he's been doing at night ever since he went to Melbourne keeps him planned out twenty-four hours a day, because the job is even busier than the one in Sydney.

Card from Russell. How do I spend my time? It's about six weeks since I've seen any of the

Howards. Zoe has a lot of friends, and studying, and photography, and parties. I used to see them often, so now I miss them very much.

On Sunday I went out to visit Charles and Nicole. I hardly ever go. It's always a mistake. Mrs Howard says, 'You're a very nice young girl of high intelligence, but you will try to expand your experience into something bizarre. Young people often do, to make themselves more interesting.'

'That's rough!' Zoe was searching through a bundle of negatives, and stopped, moving her eyes sideways to look at her mother.

'Anna's a darling.' Mrs Howard kissed the top of my head. 'I'm speaking to her as I speak to you, because we're friends.'

I thought of a word I came across in the dictionary recently: *experientialism*—the doctrine that all knowledge is derived from experience. Another word I found was: *reductive*. So, anyway, I did finally go back again to Charles and Nicole last Sunday. And since I knew what to expect, nothing should have surprised me and everything did. Mrs Howard believes the Aborigines' bone-pointing ceremony can kill, because she's read about it. She would never agree that words and thoughts kill people every day.

Anna frowned, thinking of those she knew best, from whom she had escaped. It was not only what they said and did that threatened her: in their presence, she saw with their eyes, felt with their disordered feelings, suffered their anger and panic. If she could have seen no more than their skin, she might have sustained her own life in their company. But she experienced the deadly movements of impulses that were not even conscious in them. It was as though some barrier other people possessed for their own protection was lacking in her.

Catching sight of herself in the bathroom mirror the morning after the visit, she saw a shocked stranger. In the night she had slept turbulently, dreaming and waking and falling again into heavy sleep. Now, the shape of her face and the size of her eyes were startling, anguished. She looked old. By opening and stretching her eyes and mouth, by washing and drying with great vigour, she succeeded in restoring her own look before she went to the office.

•

Stephen was here for a holiday a few weeks ago. He took me to two plays and to the pictures. The foyers in the theatres looked so big, I'd have liked to move in with my suitcase. All that space empty for hours every day and night! Stephen also took me out to dinner.

He is thin and hardly ever smiles. Since one night last year when the Howards invited me to dinner, I hadn't eaten in a restaurant. Crowds! Bright lights!

Looking back at this, I see how misleading diaries are. You never write about what you think about most.

•

Every day for fairly short periods—because they are
out, driving all over the city and suburbs, calling on
customers—I see Jim or Tom in the office. Tom brought
me roses once, when he took a big order. Most times, I
make them coffee, but sometimes they make it for me.
To each other, they never speak about their families or
what-might-have-been. They talk about their company
cars, carpentering jobs at home, mortgages, garages,
fishing, the buyers they visit, and the new general
manager in Melbourne, who has manifested himself
once in our Sydney office, coming up in the lift like
Lucifer and blowing smoke from a big cigar. He was
insulting to the men, enough to make anyone cry. But
when they went out, he leaned against my desk with
tears in *his* eyes. His name is Mr Fleming.

Jim and Tom had met him before this in
Melbourne. They were summoned down for an
emergency conference. Terrific speculation in Sydney!
They told mad jokes and we stared at each other
with great colossal eyes, as if we were having a wondering competition. But they chew themselves up with
worry. When they arrived home after the conference
they raced each other in to tell me the news. All our
communications from Melbourne are by mail, and
one by one, for weeks and months, the familiar signa-
tures on letters had been disappearing. Why? We

72

wasted a lot of time pondering over all this.

So I said, 'Well, what?'

Tom just drew a finger across his throat. Every time I mentioned a name, there went the finger across his throat again. Then a deep staring silence. Well, what about the new general manager?

Tom said seriously, 'Oh, he's just a little guy. He's got this big desk, and he practically never stands up. See him sitting there, he looks normal, then he stands up and he's level with my belt!'

'No!'

'Yes, truly.' Jim joins him in a judicious shaking of heads.

'He couldn't be!'

'No. Honestly. He's a little guy like Napoleon.'

Then they laughed and laughed, and hopped and danced over the linoleum, and made more fun of him, telling incredible stories, exorcising him. In a way, because of families and mortgages, they are in his power. After his letters began to arrive for all of us, marked *Secret and Confidential*, which we read and exchanged, I understood better why black magic might be needed.

'Yes,' they nodded. 'He's a little guy like Hitler.'

Zoe used to say, 'Salesmen. I don't know how you can put up with them. Expense-account types. You see them buying each other lunches and dinners. Hear them, I should say! I don't know why you just don't expire, having to listen to them.'

'But they're not like that. I must have told you all wrong.'

'Believe me,' Zoe said, seeming very worldly wise, 'they would be, if they could.'

'*No.* They haven't even been *given* expense accounts. They're not ordinary. Stephen's a salesman, and you liked his conversation. If that's how you see everyone. But they're no more salesmen than I am whatever title Mr Fleming gives me on the taxation return.'

Zoe combed and plaited her long black hair. She looked like Pocahontas. 'I'll concede that,' she said, which I thought rather a grand way of putting it. 'But it's a tame routine for you.'

It would be dull for Zo, and it will get dull for me. But I am not bullied. No one unconsciously wishes me harm. We never quarrel. Every day we smile at each other with real liking, the two men and I, and because good-natured people are new to me, the day is well spent.

But this is not my life.

Anna paused and stared at the wall, at the square yellow weave of the curtains and, outside the window, at a rather feeble acacia full of uncritical sparrows.

She wrote:

Russell and Lily have twin daughters—Vanessa and Caroline. Though Lily wanted dozens of children, she isn't supposed to have any more. She has gone back to work already. The babies are still very small. Stephen and Russell write to each other, but it was Zoe who told me this in a letter from Paris. She has graduated and gone away now. Why do all the people you like have to be somewhere else? But Paris! The postcards and photographs Zoe has sent home! They make me feel I have never seen a building or a street. Who wouldn't be there? You could admire any one of them for months on end. Zoe belongs there. She says she is deliriously busy, deliriously happy. And I am jealous—or would be, if I could want to be Zoe. All that has happened feels necessary. I can't picture it different. I would not want to be someone else.

•

The other tenants in this house are two middle-aged married couples, two men like grandfathers, four single women—or women who live alone—and who all seem to be about forty. We say little bits to each other.

Mr Howard came in to see me one evening. He misses Zoe. In a few weeks' time, they are having a party for some students and young people to keep the house warmed up. I'm invited, but have nothing to wear. Though I write everything down in the account book, I can't save up. By the time you put down rent, fares, food, shoe repairs, soap and toothpaste, haircuts and some dry-cleaning, there isn't anything over. The dentist. New shoes. Harder than physics. Tom says financially he is going out backwards. I know what he means. However, other people talk so much about money, especially when they have it, that I have decided not to.

Determined to avoid the subject, Anna nevertheless had thoughts less easy to control. Someone so recently freed from a lifelong siege could not be imprisoned by poverty. But tightly restricted and hampered, she knew she was. Resolutely, she expelled such ideas. Human beings soared or withered away without reference to bank accounts. The inclinations were inborn; she had no intention of withering.

Just the same, she goggled mentally at the obscurity of one person's circumstances to another when she was advised to buy, to go and see, to eat. She always answered, 'Yes, I must do that.'

•

Neglect. Poor diary, you look as though you were written in another century.

In the office, for instance—to begin with what I care about least, though I do care—Jim has gone. He's in hospital. So conscientious and keen, he has been abused and baited by Mr Fleming till he has broken up completely. He was fragile. He had feelings. Now he's under sedation. I pity men having to support wives and children and put up with the Mr Flemings because of it. What is it about someone genuine that makes other people want to crucify him in some tiny-seeming way? Someone has probably written the reason down in a book. But no one takes any notice, if we *do* know.

As for the other news—the Howards gave their party, and I wore a dress bought with birthday money from Stephen. There were thin high beautiful clouds and the air was different from town air. Mrs Howard said we could smell pittosporum, lemon blossom, prunus, wallflower, and I forget what else. The gardener contradicted her. She said he always does, and he ought to know. The party started at eleven and lasted into the night.

I met David Clermont. He is a flute player, and also teaches the flute. He plays with a small group. Anyone who knows about music thinks they are very good. He is thirty-one, and we are getting married in six weeks' time.

Anna, who had kissed the cold walls of the house she lived in as a child, who had kissed polished wood, the passing nurses and housekeepers, her sad uncle, her brother, who even quite lately had spread her arms over the grass and loved the whole continent, could not, though she believed herself willing, do more than admire and respect this man who had appeared from nowhere on the Howards' plushy lawn.

He is a fine person, she wrote, quoting, pushing her lips forward in dismay. *He knows what I feel and seems satisfied. He is a positive person.*

Pressed to come early to the party to see letters and photographs from abroad, Anna sat on a garden seat in the shade, letters read, playing with the cat. David had approached and sat beside her. Within minutes, she recognised that she was inordinately liked. Afterwards, she was to ask distractedly, 'But what did I say? What did I say?' Some accidental word of hers had acted as a hook. She would willingly have disavowed it. His wonderful attention made her feel tired, and almost harassed. Yet he was so nice. If all things had been equal, if it hadn't already been too late in a way, this could have mattered more.

David asked what objection she had to being 'liked'—the word she insisted on.

She could only look. She had the sensation, common to all caught up in a one-sided love affair, that he was trapped by some illusion of his own making. She wanted to warn him. 'Now Zoe knows all about music, but I'm—quite ignorant.' And then, because he noticed her abstraction and languor, she added, 'And she's never tired.'

He half-complained, for it was partly this he loved in her, 'How can someone of your age be so unfathomable to me?'

She wrote:

Friends and relations rejoice. I have done something popular, and clever, they seem to feel. David is immensely likeable and not a bit poor. So no one need worry about me again, or remind me of my place.

She wrote: *I wish*—
    And crossed it out.
    She wrote: *I hope*—
    And crossed it out.
    She wrote in very small letters, as though she meant to hide them even from herself: *Goodbye.*

PART TWO

In her mother's room, half-lying across the bed, Zoe pulled an awkward-looking book from the pile on the table beside her. Press cuttings. Her left hand held the cover open. Already her fingerprints would have smudged her mother's, blotting them out. Soon, from all the books, all the furniture and door handles, from everything everywhere, her mother's would be obliterated and never reappear, even though just hours ago she had breathed in this room.

Consciously, Zoe breathed. Minutes before, she had arrived from Europe, stunned by the flight, stunned to be told she was a day too late. Her head was a labyrinth of pain; she was aware of nausea and stiffness, but not really of the presence of her self. Downstairs, her father and Russell and the others were behaving well. Soon, she would be obliged to emerge, though everyone said rest for the funeral tomorrow.

It was raining. Winter here, summer in Paris. Zoe stared

through the open window at the straight lines of rain. Over there, she had described Australian winters with new-minted, dazzling skies. The rain. The very rain that fell a thousand years ago; the rain that fell on everyone who ever lived. She had a second's prompting to go outside and stand in it, but there were the stairs and people and possibly complex explanations.

In the book lying open on the bed, she saw several photographs of herself. *Zoe Howard in Paris Nightspot. Joseph Stranger and Friend. Zoe Howard on Film Set. Australian Girl with Winning Poster.*

There was the much-reproduced face of the Neapolitan urchin, now at school somewhere, a haunted face that went all over Europe, over most of the world. Money was collected for the victims of war and poverty.

Girl Photographer Parachutes into Middle East War Zone. Her mother had written, asking, 'Was that necessary?'

'Of course not,' she wrote back. 'But it was someone's bright idea. I came down (more or less) at the air terminal, far, far from any shooting. Have no fear, and don't believe anything you read in the papers. I have already been admonished by mail by Russell, for risking my life in an unworthy cause—i.e. publicity-seeking and money-making in a tragic area. It was only a commission dreamed up by a crazy friend in need of cash, but the pictures weren't bad and did no harm. Russell is probably right, but it's done now. I've admitted to being reprehensible.'

Another page fell open under her hand. Glossy photographs of private life. There was one taken when she and Joseph first met, years ago. There they sat at some café table,

Joseph looking sad, bearish, bulky, when in fact he had more facets than the Kohinoor diamond, very few of them sad or bearish. They had had a crackling quarrel that morning, Zoe remembered—her fault, some hours past, and Joseph was explaining her to herself since he was so much older and wiser, and had once been more famous than he was at present.

'You like opposition too well, my darling.'

'I rise to it, and I always shall.' Obstinately.

'But that's a very dangerous stand, and not sensible, either. See how'—he took the nearest hand and traced its lines with his forefinger, making her shiver—'if I were a cold-hearted and unscrupulous person, instead of my benevolent self, I could manoeuvre you into any frame of mind.'

Said nothing, breathed fiercely, snatched hand away.

'Wild girl. Wild girl.' He patiently took back the hand. 'I'm too—interested—in you to take advantage of you by trickery.' Looking into eyes. 'But you, ungrateful girl, don't value restraint and tact. Don't even realise. Don't even hear. I look in your eyes and see—storm, storm. Not Zoe considering Joseph's statements. Not even Zoe thinking about something else, but Zoe—storm, storm.'

Tried to pull hand away, but he held it tight.

'No. You're not going to throw something at me. We're too close together at the table, and it would be boring.' He shook his head, and turned the captive hand over and smoothed the palm with his thumb, making her shiver again, sighing slightly.

'This way of yours—I hope it isn't instinctive. It would weary us. I hope it's only youth, lack of experience, an inclination you will grow out of, or some silly habit you've picked up from your smart young friends.'

'Will you stop talking like my father? *Not* that my father would ever—'

He continued, a very large, grown-up man. 'If you were only—*storm*, I should not be so very concerned. To be young, spoilt, with a face and body, and little bits of temperament borrowed from people older than yourself, is not so unusual. Even to be intelligent, talented—there are many such people. And that is still not very much.'

With atrocious confidence. 'I don't believe any of those things are so boring to you.'

'If you were only that, we'd never have known each other so long as this. Fiery? That's not such a remarkable thing to be. The most ordinary thing in the world. No, you're more exceptional than that. You must do yourself justice, Zoe. While you are so vain, you do not even start to comprehend what you are. Do you know how I think of you?'

Then suddenly, in a trance, quite silent, hand in his, night approaching, drifts of chestnut leaves piling in the gutters, crunching underfoot, extraordinary Paris faces passing, there was happiness being given like sweetness on a spoon. Joseph took the hand he held in his two hands and kissed it and placed it on his knee.

A long time ago. More than five years since she left Sydney and the harbour, the stone house, parents and friends. Joseph had a wife in America, an aged mother in Rome, and a flickering career as a film director. None of that mattered much to her. It was all play. Although at this age—twenty-five and some months—she should have felt herself deep into her life, and experienced, she felt instead that it had only been a game.

In Roman history, Zoe had been amused, not by the antics of the infamous Clodius, but by the description of him as 'a young gay liver' and 'a debauchee'. She had wondered how gay and debauched one might have to be to qualify for such titles. Now, when she could have expected to have a clearer opinion about such matters, she believed that there were as many aspects to vice as there were stars in the sky, and that quantities of them had nothing to do with sex. A lack of mutuality, absence of tender feeling, were obscene, but nothing else. In every state of life these lacks and disparities seemed the evils from which most sadness stemmed. And yet, in spite of having learned as much as this, Zoe seemed to herself still to be waiting for the real beginning of her life. She had failed at nothing.

Sitting up, she let the book fall shut. Any moment now her mother would come in and she would be nineteen or seventeen. She would smile; her mother would look bedazzled and loving. Under the press-cutting book, she saw a smaller volume. Family photographs. Russell, Lily and the twins. Grandparents, now dead. Zoe could just remember the muted sensation of their going. It had seemed unaffecting, quite natural and unmoving, that grandparents should die. They had lived in other cities, were unfamiliar except in anecdote. As they dropped away, her mother and father showed no great sign, determined to cast no shadows on their children, not to be overthrown by emotion. They had each other.

Anna's wedding. Zoe studied this with a swooning mind. David's face looked large and smooth, his eyes lively and intelligent, his mouth sensitive and magnanimous, ready to smile. They were married for eighteen months. Then out of the blue she had heard that he was in hospital with some difficult-to-diagnose disease. In six weeks he was dead, Anna a young widow. He was only thirty-three.

Till now there had seemed to be so much time. Since time stops, the world—which has been waiting for you in particular—stops when you arrive and grow up. It must be some inbuilt trickery, some necessary blindness, that makes us think so. And she had felt herself scarcely launched, still only standing up to her ankles in the ocean. When all the while human beings disappeared constantly from view. Likeable men of thirty-three. Her *mother*.

'Come on, sweetheart. Don't stay up here by yourself.' Her father stood behind her with a hand on her shoulder. She twisted round to look up at him. He had lost weight.

He said, 'Anna's downstairs talking to Russell and Lily. She and Stephen have come over to see you.'

'Oh, yes.' Zoe paused, then rose to her feet. She swayed and held her father's arm.

The room was lit like a stage directed to represent the desert at midday, though it was some unidentifiable hour of night. Numerous persons of a mind-jerking familiarity (like the crooked wooden telegraph poles, like the weeds, strongly calling and signalling to her through the car window on the drive from Mascot, like the sweet breath of the continent blowing through her mother's room) sat about or walked in and out on errands, making her think again of the stage, of actors waiting for a rehearsal to begin. Apart from her family, Lily's mother and father were there, Uncle John from Melbourne, the Pattersons, and the Blakes, friends since childhood, Janet Bell, her mother's best friend, Tony Merson from Biology, and finally, Anna—now Anna Clermont—and Stephen Quayle.

After embraces, Zoe sat down expecting her mother to come in swiftly and switch off half the lights, making the room habitable and intimate and like itself. Everyone murmured apologetically about her death. Minute after minute, she failed to appear. Zoe's head continued to swoon. Her heart fell into hallucinated regions while the gathering, intent on cheering up, questioned her about the wide world.

Almost for the first time in her life, Zoe felt herself at the mercy of circumstances. She was *never* overborne, yet she was overborne, letting herself be talked to, meek, unable to assert her will, or even to be certain what that was. All the things ever said about death were true. Like a light going out. If her mother came in the door now, turning off all the lamps, still the glow from her presence would make the room visible.

'We were always seeing pictures of you taking pictures.' Tony Merson eyed her intensely, giving the impression that his glance was taking a hundred tiny photographs for future reference. 'You know, the parachute one, and in the refugee camps with the kids. Living dangerously,' he said, taking further pictures with his eyes.

Still her mother waited outside the door, refrained from smiling, from saying, 'It's like the Hotel Australia!' and banishing the remorseless, shadowless glare of a public place.

Zoe said, 'From here it doesn't seem worth much.' Across the room, Russell and Anna were standing together.

Then Stephen was in front of her. 'You should look older than you do,' she told him soberly.

'How so?' He sat next to her on the sofa. Tony Merson gave her hand a valedictory squeeze and moved off from his confidential perch beside her.

'So much has happened, so far away. Like science fiction. You return from outer space unchanged and find your contemporaries ancient.'

Again she looked in the direction of the door. Someone had left it open, exposing among the bright angles of copper, flower arrangements, paintings, no person. No one. Zoe studied the distant hall for a few seconds. She said without expression, 'I feel she's in another room. I keep wanting to look through the house to see what she's doing...And you, Stephen, still the boyish anarchist, still young, upsetting all my notions. Are you as wrapped up in brown paper and string?' She felt her head jerk involuntarily away from him.

'More than ever. But in Sydney now, with a secretary and access to the top-secret files. All that's lacking is a hotline to Washington and Moscow. A success story.' Tallish, spare of frame, as he was years ago. His clothes were better, and his barber knew how to cut hair. But he had altered at less superficial levels, too; had an ease of manner distinctly absent when they first met. Most noticeably, he looked directly at the person he was talking to.

Zoe forced herself to converse as though she had merely come home for a visit. 'I've heard of other things...Science. Your degree...Yes, you went away to Melbourne. I remember thinking you did that on purpose.'

'There wasn't much choice, but I thought I'd better get out.'

She stated, 'Because of me,' and he nodded. When he began to speak again, Zoe found herself watching his teeth, small and well-shaped, as familiar as her own. 'That was a pity,' she said, not noticing that she interrupted him. 'But you've changed.'

From time to time Zoe continued to glance at the open door, expecting a doctor to appear, saying, 'Everything is going to be all right. In a few days she'll be up and about.' When no one made any such announcement, when her mother chose to stay away, and stay away, she turned with untiring patience back to Stephen, her expression curiously fixed. To be seen by *them*, the powers of the world, to have limitless patience to spend on her mother's survival was essential.

Stephen said, 'You aren't the same, either.'

Zoe looked into his eyes coldly for a second or two. 'Well, I'm not like this, if that's what you think. However I seem now, it's not what I'm like.'

His interest, once so desired, now so unsurprisingly given, made him no less alien to her. By allowing her eyes to pass deliberately over the quiet groups of actors standing in clusters or turning chairs to form islands, she reminded him of the occasion. Death. Her mother. But how inept he was, after all! Tactful, instructive movements of the eyes were wasted on him.

Self-conscious but unconscious, discontented but apparently passive in his discontent, since he was still involved in the sale of packaging. A faulty man, sensitive and obtuse. He had taken off his glasses. Her eyes focussed on his hands as in a gigantic close-up—thin, long-fingered. The contents of her head swooped and zoomed as though the house rocked on its foundations. Feeling sick, she glanced away from Stephen to the room and its quiet inhabitants. And frail, and in fearful danger, they looked to her.

'Could you get me something to drink? Who's taking care of all these people? Didn't Russell and Lily move in to help? Nothing very hospitable seems to be happening. It's not like our house.'

'They've all eaten hours ago. You have a drink there.' He nodded at the low table in front of them.

But now there was a stirring in the room as though the star or the producer had been spotted approaching from behind the scenes. There were voices in the hall. Mrs Perkins came in abruptly, eyes in mottled face hunting out Mr Howard, who stood with Lily's father. Zoe and Stephen held each other's gaze to listen more attentively to her message.

'Mr Proctor's here about the funeral.'

•

'You're a pest, Zo,' Russell shouted after her.

'Same to you.'

'If you just want to drown yourself, why sink Gavin's tub?'

'It's insured.'

'For God's sake!'

'What did you say?'

'I said bugger off,' Russell muttered, watching her shoot out into the harbour. It was a month after the funeral, mid-winter, the sailing season well and truly over. The sky was violet and charcoal and half past eleven in the morning. Finding that Russell and her father had long ago sold their boats, Zoe demanded that Russell borrow one for her. After a telephone call, they charged down the hill, arguing into the wind.

'Don't do it.'

'I shall. I will. I'm going to. I want to.'

'Everyone knows you're intrepid, Zo. No need to prove anything.'

'I never knew anyone with less talent for irony.'

'Satire. With just as little success, of course.'

'I'm taking that leaky-looking thing out.' She lowered her chin slightly, and looked up at him with a defiant expression that had nothing to do with sailing. It was Stephen. It was Stephen. They all suddenly tried to make nothing of him, silently resisted him, opposed her. Without speaking, they pressed opinions on her.

True, her poor father had been too busy making arrange-ments to go overseas to throw in his weight on their side, but everyone else, down to the remotest connection, had gone about just not shuddering at the sound of Stephen's name. She had seen him almost every evening. Her return booking to Paris had been cancelled, and although the ticket had not yet been cashed, it seemed to be fearfully assumed that she would stay. There had been two telephone calls from Joseph, and letters and cables about work. Most of her belongings were on the other side of the world. But none of this was the point. While she and Russell inspected the atoms of each other's eyes, her compressed and coded thoughts, banked tighter every day, exploded between them.

'I've always had the impression that he was your great friend. We could have recited his virtues off by heart from the day you met. And all the time you were away you exchanged letters, and now you're back there's this printing press and you might be partners. And *yet* when you see whatever it is you see—about *us*—there's all this dubiousness. And I think, "What is it that makes Stephen acceptable as a lifelong friend and partner, and impossible as—" Or perhaps it's something about me? But anyway, I don't care what you think. And, God knows how, he hasn't noticed the absence of enthusiasm. Even Anna—' she broke off bitterly, and turned to stare at the heaving water. The boatshed beside which they stood, banged and rattled as though working up to take off.

'Zo...' Russell pulled at her waterproof sleeve consolingly. 'It's nothing. We worry about you. I don't know what it is. He's not easy. You're so different from each other. You don't seem to have much in common.'

'What on earth do you mean? You can't know either

of us, if you think that.'

Hands shoved in his pockets, Russell poked at a few stones with the toe of his shoe. 'Your life in Paris was *right*. It was your line. You were slaving at something that was important to you—'

'—Joseph slaved and so did everyone near him. What he does *is* important. I'm not the only one who thinks so.'

'That's all I'm saying—good work, good company. Your letters made me envious.'

They both laughed. Then Zoe scoffed, 'Envious? You? Tone it down a little. But I was in good company,' she agreed, momentarily sombre. Her spirit revived. 'There are people I'll hate not seeing again. Didn't even say a proper goodbye. But the fact that I may choose to let all this go should convince you I'm serious.'

Russell's blue eyes contemplated her. 'You couldn't sit at home here—a suburban lady on charity committees, having fashionable lunches with other ladies, and spending your talents on your clothes.'

She side-stepped and attacked. 'You talk about not having much in common! Who could be less alike than you and Lily? Lily should have married a professor. If you're not an academic, she thinks you might as well cut your throat. You liked it in London in the thick of things: she likes it here with her family, and the prospect of being a big fish in her department when she stops being a mother. But the reason you give is, quote, that this is the best place in the world to bring up children, unquote. What a cliché!'

There was a brief pause.

'Leaving aside my non-existent problems, there's only one thing in everyone's mind—could you settle down here again? That's all. I like it. It suits me. But it's the far side of the moon.'

Zoe was watching him with a sort of dreamy, abstracted interest. He never seemed to get angry. Anger was something he could do without. A gust of wind blew her hair up and over her face. Roughly she smoothed it down and plaited it. 'Look at that sky. Set for the Second Coming. All those portentous rays. Any minute—trumpets!' There was something enchanting and winning and touching about her, and she knew it, and Russell knew it, though exactly what it was at that moment he would have been hard put to say. A sweetness at the core. Something irritating and undeserved like that.

He said, 'You're more likely to hear the Last Post on a bugle if you take that boat out. Come on. Let's go back.'

'I've got things to think about,' she said, searching her pockets. 'You wouldn't have any rubber bands?' She showed him the unravelled ends of her plaits.

Sighing, he patted himself over. 'No. No ribbons either.'

'Then push off, darling. But give us a hand with this first. And if anything happens—remember, I love you all.'

Five minutes later, she shot out into the bay, shouting, 'Airborne!'

Russell trudged up the hill. 'I couldn't watch,' he said to Lily, who was in the kitchen preparing for a dinner party. She looked up and smiled and licked some sauce from the side of a forefinger. She nodded at the table where Vanessa and

Caroline, like miniature replicas of their Aunt Zoe, were rolling out scraps of pastry, moulding them into balls, then pounding them flat with baby fists. 'Jesus says—Je-sus says—you have to share that rolling pin, Vanessa.'

'What happened to yours?' her mother asked.

'Lost. All gone.'

Russell found it under the table and restored it to the owner.

'Stephen rang. I told him what was happening, and he said he was going after her. There's some boat he can take, better than Gavin's.'

With a groan, Russell sat down at the end of the table. 'Where's my aqua-lung? Don't tell me any more. It's like Madame Butterfly—all rushing to the water's edge.'

'Well, not quite.'

'They're insane. It's only the filthiest day of the year. They'll have everything from water spouts to tidal waves out there. I wonder if someone else would like to go for a sail?'

'Oh yes, Daddy! Yes, yes.' The twins slipped off their chairs and ran to him, rubbing pastry into his trousers and sweater and hair as they swarmed over him. 'Go for a sail. Take us, Daddy.'

'Well,' Lily said, reasonably, when he opened his eyes at her.

Zoe clung to the tiller like someone riding a steer in a rodeo. The light was now peculiarly sulphurous and the wind was noisy as an opera with all the principals assembled, shrieking over the death of the hero. How close to the water she was!

And yet she seemed to be thinking of something else while she fumbled with soaking rope and wood and hair. Some shipping, foreign cargo freighters, lay at anchor, deserted; otherwise, the harbour was stripped of life. It occurred to Zoe that she might be in danger, yet she had an impression of being locked away safe and secure with all eternity in which to reach conclusions.

With tremendous speed she reviewed everyone she had ever known—the lucky, invulnerable. Even Russell, who should know better, was a light-minded man. Even this month, with so much sadness, he sang to her on the telephone, told terrible jokes against himself, bought presents for no special reason and behaved, generally, in a foolish way. And in Paris, Joseph, who had so little judgment that he considered himself in the midst of some deathless love affair. For a man of that age to be so romantic! Hard-working, accomplished, perhaps even an artist, but basically weak, she decided harshly. To love more than you were loved in return—how little character that showed!

Stephen. All the careful compliments from the family that fell short of accuracy. They could not admit the significance of his life because it would show them at such a disadvantage. Too bad, she thought grimly, welcoming an excuse to take up arms against the old life, returning like a warrior from the first death she had known. Well, they *would* respond to him if she had to apply thumb screws.

If they wanted to throw down challenges, she would pick them up though her life was at stake. If she had to battle colossal disapproval, they need not think she would hesitate.

When she had said this yesterday to Anna, Anna had only replied, 'Don't you ever find the people you're reacting against are paying less attention than you think? If you look decisive, people think you know what you're doing, and they're always relieved.'

'That sounds like a wise observation, Anna.' The only thing was, she had blocked out the sense of it, absolutely knowing it was nothing to her purpose. Her purpose was to feel opposed.

Yet some very small sensation that perhaps no one was daring her to fall in love with Stephen and marry him, that her defiance was directed at no one, caused her to hesitate this Sunday morning. Almost, she could feel herself checked on the brink, pricking her ears, scanning the horizon for comments and signs, testing the air for danger or promise, breasting the challenge scented everywhere.

Three sickening gulps of saltwater woke her. She heard a cry and turned. A heavy crack on the skull blacked out even the deepest spell. There was underground singing. Everything moved and heaved under her. Half-drowned, she saw Stephen and some strange man leaning over her.

So be it.

Stephen was shouting. She said, 'I wanted to think. What's this—a ferry?' Then she was sick. 'Is Gavin's boat all right?' And she was sick again. Stephen held her as she leaned over the tossing sea.

Dried and warmed and fed and combed, three hours later she was sitting up in bed receiving visitors.

'Stephen saved my life, and we're getting married practically tomorrow. Or did I say that before?'

Lily gave the entranced face a severe look. 'You've said it ten times. Considering that your life needn't have *been* in danger...We were down at the beach. Do you think Russell would let you drown?'

Zoe turned away. 'It was a sign,' she said childishly, into the pillow, and two childish tears came to her eyes. She felt irrational, and right. It was not the first time she had accepted what was thrown in her path as a sign from the universe, but this most momentous acceptance erased all the others.

Russell came to the door. 'Dr Todd said he's given her an injection. She'll be out to it in five minutes.'

Lying very still to hear what else might be imparted, she heard Lily say in a low voice, 'I hope she's back to normal in the morning.'

'Knowing Zo's normal...'

She smiled, and slept.

•

Dear Joseph,
Darling Joseph,
My dear Joseph,

Dear God! If she couldn't even decide what to call him!

Dear Joseph,

Thank you for your letters, and thank you for arranging to have everything packed and shipped over. I'm sorry not to have written sooner. How much did it cost?

Or, how I won golden opinions for tact, charm and graciousness. Thank you, like a business letter, then money, as if she'd hired him to do a job. If you can take the trouble to remember someone deeply, you can write human letters, otherwise you write form letters that could go to anyone, and read like a draught from a refrigerator.

Dear Joseph,

You ask for news. We've been married for five months, as you know from my other note. We're living in the house I inherited from my mother, at the end of that little beach I've described to you. Russell and Lily (whom you'll remember after that famous visit) and their two small daughters have the old house. My father went to South Africa some time ago, and is giving lectures there. He is so outspoken he'll end up in prison.

Russell has turned renegade now that they're back here—that is, Lily wanted him to winkle himself into one of the universities here, after winkling him out of the university there to bring the children home to her parents. He was working on some project in London, but has developed anti-sociological scruples for reasons I haven't been able to plumb. Lily is having seizures. When I tell Russell he is too vain to look at people in the light of other men's theories, he agrees with me.

So, after the sadness and turmoil of my mother's illness and death, and after they had moved into our old place, he was prevailed on by a friend who wanted to sell a Dickensian printery. (The machines are the best, but the building has little wooden staircases running all over it.) He (and I) then persuaded Stephen to resign from his uncongenial work, and they are now partners in this eccentric printery-cum-publishing thing that they know very little about.

Because Lily couldn't face leaving the children with a housekeeper, she has been translating various pieces at home—German. She asked me to help her, then we had to ask other friends if they could take on extra work, and now we have an office in town. We have a woman there to answer the phone. Most of the time, Lily and I work at home.

Apart from this, Stephen and I had the house brought nearer the heart's desire, by a team of Italian builders and painters, then furnished it, and I'm marvellously happy. It should be illegal to be so happy, and possibly is.

What piffle! Zoe thought, looking back at the letter. What a very false tone! Because he wouldn't want to hear all this about

Russell and Stephen and domestic details. And it all amounted to an elaborate padding in which she could insert the vital news, the only news, *I am marvellously happy*. She felt a tremendous need to say it, and an equally deep, quite opposite need to be secret and private.

Vacantly she gazed out over the garden at the sea through its screen of leaves, its fringe of sand, grass and boatsheds. It was hard to remember Joseph. He was so far away. He had asked for a letter. That was how it had turned out, with all these busy details leading to her happiness. She had camouflaged and protected and made light of it all the way through, only to expose it entirely at the very end, like a magician, pattering on about trifles then whipping off the sheet under which birds and flowers had come to life.

She was using Joseph. He would notice, but he would make allowances. He always had. But the propriety of mentioning her happiness...

Briefly, she fell to considering her extraordinary good fortune, something so far above anything that had ever been conceived, that she lived always now at two levels—the practical, visible one, where she performed deeds in the world, swiftly, without effort, and the other real level, where she lived with Stephen in a state she could not describe even to herself, only experience, a flawless *now*.

Suddenly angry, as though the absent Joseph had debated all this with her, she turned back to the page. How could *he* understand? He had only known her before.

Stephen is a very complex person, and although
superficially we might seem quite different, we are very
much alike.

She continued to write rapidly about herself and Stephen, then
turned her head at a sound. 'Anna! Read this. I'm going to fix
the sprinkler. What you never realise about owning property is
the way someone has to look after it.'

They kissed, and Anna took the letter. 'I'm early. I thought
you'd be out here.'

'Lovely. Gives us time before the others get here.' With a
bright glance, she ran down the steps to the garden and disappeared round the side of the house.

'Are you going to send this?' Anna asked, holding the letter
up as Zoe returned.

'Why? Yes. When it's finished.' But Zoe looked at the
other girl, startled. 'What's wrong with it?'

Anna's eyes moved about, unconcentrated. 'Well. It's *chatty*.
But you haven't mentioned him, or his work, or anyone you
both knew.' She looked at her friend. 'Would he want to hear
Stephen's praises sung?'

'Why shouldn't he? Why not?' Zoe frowned her hostility.

'If he loved you?'

'Oh—' She hesitated impatiently, looking into the past
over Anna's head. 'He only thought he did. I mean—I suppose
he did. It was good while it lasted. But he's too busy to go on
being an unrequited lover.'

Anna laughed. 'Oh, Zo!'

'You and David didn't meet him in Paris, did you? He was away. Why all the concern, then? You think I'm callous.'

'Yes. I think you're callous. I like his expression. He looks interesting. I've read interviews.'

Nodding, Zoe sat opposite Anna at the small wooden table where she had done her composing. She admitted, 'He is nice. You'd like him. But, Anna, you can't consider everyone simultaneously.'

'That's so. Oh well, then.' Anna propped an elbow on the table and cupped her face in the palm of her hand. 'I suppose he'll survive. You're right that not everyone feels so much.'

'Did I say that?' Looking puzzled, Zoe questioned a puzzled Anna, then they both laughed.

'Everything's wonderful with Stephen? I haven't seen you for ages.'

'Don't sound so sceptical. You're never very friendly towards him.' To her own amazement, Zoe's eyes filled with tears. She had become infinitely sensitive on his account, as she had never had reason to be on her own.

Anna said gently, looking at the white-painted tabletop, 'I *would* be. But he holds people off. We get on each other's nerves a bit. He's not really—'

'What?'

'Very fond of people. Except you, of course, which is all that matters.'

'No, it isn't all that matters. Don't say that.' Anxiously, Zoe rubbed her scalp with a shampooing motion for a few seconds. Abruptly, she stopped. 'Everyone'll be arriving, and I'm not even dressed. But Mrs Trent's in the kitchen. But, Anna,' she said, in a pleading lover's tone that the very thought of Stephen evoked, 'already he's changed so much. I don't want him to be anyone but himself, but he *wasn't*.' She added, looking away, eyes unfocussed, 'He's a very complex person. Nobody really understands.'

Anna let this pass in a silence also rather complex.

'But when you think of it,' Zoe went on eagerly, 'who else would go to the slavery of getting a degree part-time at night, and then not use it? He says a first degree in science only qualifies you to teach, and he'd never do that. And he couldn't see himself going on, year after year, at night, for the next one. Now he's with Russell and everything's different, but before this—all those years as a salesman! I do understand it, but it baffles me. Why should he have settled for so long, for something so—incongruous?'

Anna had given her brother thought for years, but nothing about him was new to her as it was to Zoe. She attended while Stephen's wife mused aloud.

'If he didn't intend to free himself when he *was* qualified, what did he think he was doing? Why did he think he was making that effort?'

Every day the evidence of Stephen's unparalleled disposition accumulated: it was clear in his least glance, in his every statement. Making love, eating, walking, swimming, attending dinners, parties, theatres, meetings, were all, in different degrees, ways of coming to know him. No one had the faintest comprehension! They acted as if this were just any marriage, and Stephen just anyone. Zoe now recognised, through him, that he had somehow been an emergency all his life, and that the understanding of him, and making happy of him, and finding himself for him, had to take precedence over all else.

There was nothing easy about it. Whatever he said was true, but his true statements had begun to seem like pieces of a jigsaw whose subject was a secret. They had to be recorded, then carefully held in suspense, till their place emerged. She might have asked for explanations, but why should he try to explain more than he readily could? The last desire she had was to question and grind him up into some dull reasonable thing where all could be understood by a child of five. She took it for granted that there were excellent reasons for everything he had ever done, even if she didn't know what they were.

'He had that interview with the drug company,' Anna said.

'And the man was so bloody rude! Some tin-pot executive acting like a tycoon, reading letters and fiddling with papers while the suppliant waited.'

'More like a weed than a tycoon. Wherever you've got six people working together, you're going to have at least one suffering from *folie de grandeur*.'

'Really?' Zoe took this in. 'My sheltered life. I suppose it's true. I've known some tempestuous characters. There are individuals I'd rather starve than defer to. What are you thinking? "She's never been put to the test." You Quayles! You haven't starved, either!'

Laughing, Anna agreed, 'We should be banned.'

'But wait till you see him! I'm going to get dressed. Amuse

yourself.' She stopped suddenly in the doorway and looked back at Anna with a distant awareness of her own egotism. She used Joseph, used Anna, rarely remembered to ask that part of the human race not Stephen, 'How are you?'

Excessively, even for someone in love, Zoe had found a chameleon-like capacity for fitting herself to Stephen's moods. Other people had always adjusted to *her* moods, bent their natures to please *her*, coaxed, pleaded and reasoned with *her*. They had left her glutted and spoiled, she told herself. Although, to be fair all round, she hadn't realised it at the time.

Now, her mere existence was far from enough to satisfy Stephen's standards. Almost always—total accord, zest, a perfect marriage, she assured herself. But from time to time there was a flash of silent criticism that told her Stephen had other superior visions of her to the one she presented. She discovered an ability to strive for approval. It was like finding an extra sense. She accepted correction. It was, at the very least, a novelty. Friends said, 'You're a different person.' In the ground of this different person, Stephen flourished.

In Melbourne he had had loveless associations with two older women, both unsatisfactorily married, both watching for someone richer, more ambitious, with more time to spare and a less barbed manner. Here, Zoe's task was to supply a confidence so special there seemed to be no name for it. It could only be referred to tangentially. But they knew what the trouble was *not*: it was nothing between them. Meantime, being adored, listened to, marvelled at, agreed with, gently teased, made to laugh, well fed, looked after, deferred to, entertained, relieved of the tedious chores of a bachelor's existence, seen to be lord and master of someone as noteworthy as Zoe, treated by Zoe with the profound respect of idolatrous love and the levity of a Hindu goddess—these many new experiences altered Stephen.

Dressing, Zoe thought to call some sort of warning to Anna. But what? 'He isn't completely cured yet'? As though she regarded him as somehow ill? When it was nothing like that. Combing her hair, inspecting her make-up, she could admit what barriers remained, but preferred to let the list trail off. Censure came easily to him. There was that. Malice had surprised her. But in the beautiful future...

In the sitting room, Anna bit into a salted almond and opened and folded the newspaper. Wars everywhere. Dead and wounded everywhere. Refugees everywhere. She read the reports. Scientists gloomy about the earth's chances of survival. The pages rustled over. Industrial unrest, skirt lengths, mining, recipes, finance, hairstyles—all passionately propounded like so many religions with fanatical one-eyed adherents.

World, you are too much with us.

'Eventually,' Zoe said, coming in with arms raised, still fixing her hair.

'Eventually, what?'

'I'd like Stephen to see the world,' she said defensively. 'It might make a difference.'

'Would you go back to your own work?'

'No, no. That didn't amount to much.' She spoke hurriedly and assessed the room at a glance, thinking of the evening's guests. 'Oh, I'll do something else as soon as life's settled a bit.'

'What about the Bureau? You and Lily.'

'Oh, that! Have a nut.' Zoe crunched some. 'It's mushroomed, but it's only temporary. Sitting around with dictionaries, acquiring curvature of the spine—it's a bit passive for my taste. I'm used to being with people. There used to be that feeling of everything flashing past like an express train, but now—' Suddenly spreading her arms out, she laughed. 'It's more like floating in sunshine.'

She could not even think about it, for the words to express it had been debased by having been used to mean less. With Stephen, she had fallen into eternity. Every word they uttered was an acknowledgement of this fact. 'Is it raining?' or 'Please pass the salt' were affirmations of the miraculous nature of the feeling between them. If he walked into the room unexpectedly, she would look up and, looking, not know which body she inhabited. She asked him, 'Did anyone ever die of requited love? Because I easily might. All this time, I've had the temperament of a woman who could ruin herself for love, and never knew it. With anyone else, anyone else, my life would have been disastrous.'

Joseph had called her frivolous. Her perpetual light-heartedness towards him made him pretend to suffer. He had exaggerated everything so—her mysterious fascination, his equally mysterious pain. Of course, if he sensed before she did the person she was now, the version she offered must have seemed shallow. As if anyone like that had need of her!

She cried again, 'We're marvellously happy. Great exalta-tion! You know the feeling?'

Sitting back in a corner of the sofa, Anna smiled. 'Dimly.'

A thought struggled to consciousness and the radiance faded from Zoe's face. 'Oh, hell! I suppose it's a crime to be happy. It's also, also, a much worse one to be miserable.' Shimmering with defiance and mortification, she stared at her widowed friend, remembered the displaced lover, before both of whom she was drawn to go on about her bliss. 'Have a cigarette. Have a drink,' she said, pouring large quantities of gin and firmly discarding compunction.

'I am in *favour* of happiness,' Anna declared, accepting the overflowing glass. 'Cross my heart. Never be miserable.'

'I promise that,' Zoe said, and drank. Then glancing up, she saw Stephen standing in the doorway. They surveyed each other, then approached slowly as though taking part in a ritual. Leaving aside Anna's restricting presence, there were the messages to read. Zoe had to understand without being told all that had happened during his hours of absence. The signals never seemed to be the same two days in succession. Being married to him, Zoe thought, was like taking a perpetual intel-ligence test. (And she had once contributed to conversations in which *film-making* was discussed as a difficult creative art!) Without speaking, they kissed and stood together.

Stephen turned to his sister, and she jumped up and they gave each other a quick hug. 'How's Anna? Very glamorous, whatever else! Where's John?'

They studied each other, stepping back.

'Arriving later. You look well.'

Pretending to flex his muscles, he gave a smile such as Anna had never received from him before.

'Lily thinks the twins have caught measles. She and Russell can't come,' he told them.

'Damn! What a nuisance!' Handing Stephen a drink, she added, 'If Lily heard that...'

'She'd scalp you.' He walked over to look down through the trees to the beach. 'Still someone in the water. I'll have a shower.' Taking a gulp of whisky, he turned back to the women again.

'John will be disappointed to miss Russell,' Anna commented. 'Their last meeting changed his life. He was inspired.'

'John?' Zoe asked.

'Need you ask?'

'No need to ask who provides inspiration.' Stephen finished his drink and met no one's eye. 'There'll be only one star tonight, instead of two. And Russell gave me another message. Your mother's friend, Ellen: he saw somewhere that she'd died.'

'Really?' Her forehead wrinkling, Zoe stared at him, then at Anna. 'I remember her quite well. She had a German husband. She always used to say, "Hans and I can't go on like this, Alice. Something must change." He's possibly dead now, too. Not that they were so old.' Zoe looked at her own husband. He had gained weight; the bones of his face were covered; his skin was tanned and healthy. She said vaguely, 'But this could never have been the change Ellen wanted.'

Sliding ice about in her empty glass, Anna said, 'We never understand how little time there is. This is what you want to say to people—that there's no time for lies. You have to decide and act now. This might be all the time there is. They don't seem to understand. Or else they don't care.'

Zoe had no feeling of there being any shortage of time. What was Anna thinking about? Or was she just interesting herself by playing the melancholy young widow? This was the wrong moment for pensive utterances—a gorgeous, glowing evening with the beach down there suddenly deserted and the sand turning cool and white, and the calm harbour a bay of light, and the trees beatified by the late sunlight.

'Let's not think about life's profounder meanings *now*.' Zoe spun round so that her long dress rippled out. 'If I'm to be the solitary star without Russell—*and* cook, with Mrs Trent's help—I can't afford to brood, and neither can my husband, nor my chiefest guest. Russell must have given you that news about Ellen to jinx us.' She put an arm round Stephen's waist, and they smiled into each other's eyes. The bell rang.

'I'll vanish.' He grabbed his briefcase and headed for the stairs.

Zoe looked after him. The bell rang again. In the instant of flying off to answer it, she turned to Anna with an expression at one triumphant and pleading. You see? He walks. He talks. He listens indulgently while I say silly things. He lets eight strange people invade his house. Physically, in every way, he's a new man. Is this not all very amazing and wonderful?

Understanding what was required of her, Anna gave several small congratulatory and affectionate nods of her head.

•

'I don't wish you any harm, Stephen, but I wish the printery would go broke.' Lily spoke with her usual vehemence and her eyes looked resentful, but as always her voice diverted attention from the subject. The slightly hoarse quality, the beautifully pure enunciation, the resonance and constant surprise of its range, left sensitive ears quite dazed with delight.

Out on the verandah of the old Howard house at the opposite end of the beach from the Quayles' place, Stephen and his sister sipped their iced drinks and listened.

In parenthesis Lily told them, 'Russell's out distributing good cheer to aged characters in Balmain. He found them when he was taking the cleaner's sick pay over one night. Went to the wrong address. He found this little nest of metho drinkers or whatever they are. He's always making amends to the world for something a lunatic couldn't call his fault. I'm sure that as a child he did it for all sorts of reasons connected with being better off and brainier and more likeable than other people. He's like some angel of God consoling us sinners for not being perfect. Like him,' she added bitterly, but with an air of ambivalence that gave her the freedom to change moods instantaneously.

Turning her head aside, Anna defended him. 'Poor Russell!'

Stephen protested, 'I don't see many signs that he thinks he's perfect.'

'It's just that his disciples do.' Lily drank and put her glass down on the ledge. 'His parents had to be consoled for something or other. It's hard to see *what* when you think of their lives. Then the boys who drowned. That meant something else. And there were *their* parents. He still sees them. Then the camp. What he has to do to make up for that! He feels too much. Men oughtn't to be like that. Most men aren't. It's supposed to be a feminine quality—feeling, but I've never known any woman with this pathological condition. It cripples him,' she said, not to be silenced by her visitors' withdrawn and troubled expressions. 'He notices too much. I tell him it's inflation. I tell him he's been swallowed by an archetype. He laughs.' Breathless and flushed, she challenged them to contradict her.

Looking down, Stephen scratched his ear.

Lily said bracingly, 'I can see you're about to defend him, man-like.'

'If I knew what the charge was—' Taking off his spectacles and mangling them with his long fingers so that when they were resumed he saw Lily's face through a blur of whorls, he added disarmingly, 'If I knew what the charge was, I'd doubt it.'

'What unhelpful discretion! Just what I expected.'

'But using technical terms on him!' Anna ate a maraschino cherry, tranquil as a saucer of cream, nervously unable to decide if this sounded a normal reproachful thing to say. She only knew that too great a silence might not seem normal, either. Lily had always been inclined to use words like 'motivated' and 'sibling rivalry' and 'affective blunting': the habit seemed pathetic and dangerous to Anna, a way Lily had of putting a distance between herself and people. So, 'Technical terms,' she said.

'Oh, don't worry about that.' Lily moved in her chair so violently that combs and hairpins dropped out of her hair. Stephen leaned over to pick them up. 'Thanks. He doesn't care. He announces himself to me on the phone as a representative of the Great Earth Mother. You can laugh.'

Stephen gave a small envious smile. 'It isn't easy to get him down.'

But, clearly, all lightness in Lily today was superimposed on a deep-rooted grievance. It was difficult to know how seriously angry she was, except by the fact that she had scarcely been known to mention Russell's name in his absence, much less to complain of him like this.

'Have some more before all the ice melts. It's Sunday. We're allowed to be lazy. The children are asleep with their temperatures, poor lambs. They can have Zo's nice pudding that you brought over when they wake up.'

Handing over the replenished glasses, she sat down again on the long wooden chair and put her feet up. She was wearing Roman sandals, white trousers and a blue shirt. With her elbows on the arms of the chair, she held her drink firmly in both hands, and stared over it unsmiling.

'I hate the printery,' she said again. '"But why that?" I say to Russell. "Why not a tobacco kiosk, or a cake shop?" If he wants to turn a penny and doesn't care how.'

Stephen was beginning to glower. Not meeting her eye, he said, 'There's a slight difference. You can reach people through a press. When the newsletter starts, you might change your mind.'

More than most, he resented criticism. Though it was crystal clear that Lily's attacks were directed at her husband, Anna could see from the repressive, warning blankness of his expression that Stephen had managed to feel himself the object of abuse. She sympathised with him, but hoped they could escape before he said something unforgettably disagreeable.

'I've heard that one. "The press that changed the world." Well, it won't happen.' Lily fell silent. With a fingernail she scratched at a thread on the padded chair cover. 'He's wasting his life deliberately. I don't know why.'

Anna appraised the smooth old tiles paving the verandah, then looked out over the many fresh and sumptuous greens of the garden, silent, silent. Her head rang and echoed with statements. Of all people, she had most right to speak! Watching the trees, she felt in the pocket of her dress and, fetching out her sunglasses, covered her eyes.

With his arched fingers meeting just under his mouth, Stephen said stiffly, 'We're under the impression it's doing well.'

'Oh, you'll do *well*,' Lily said violently. 'You're rapid learners. But that's not exactly the point. The point is you should both be doing the work you're equipped to do. (I'm not really speaking about you, Stephen: what you do is your own affair.) But Russell has special knowledge, special training, like you.

And he was very well thought of.'

Anna dared to say, 'Perhaps the feeling and noticing aren't such a handicap, then? I've worked in less salubrious places than you, Lily—I'm not boasting!' she protested, half-laughing. 'Not from choice! But I came to know quite different people, and— so, I can't think of these qualities of Russell's as defects.'

'They aren't,' Stephen said decisively.

Their unanimity pulled her up. She waved away some small insect cruising in front of her face, and almost apologetically grimaced. 'I never discuss him. Pretty contemptible. Especially in front of you, Anna,' she added, somehow keenly, as though she had found a reason to apologise twice over. 'Because you're not even a member of the family.'

'*No*,' Anna agreed, with polite enthusiasm.

Lily went on, 'Anyway, having gone so far, I might as well tell you what led to the press. I was persuading him to come home, but *not* to give up his. . .' She sighed. 'In London, he was one of a team working with a supposedly great man. They were studying odd pockets of the population. It was all rather hush-hush. You know what these special projects are like. In due course there was going to be a great book about these unfortunate specimens.'

'What sort of?' Anna asked.

With a pretence of smoothing her forehead and hair, Lily put both hands to her head. 'Oh, Lord! Let's just say a grievous cross-section. The idea was that good would come of it all in the end, and it might have. But two members of the team were—I don't know what you'd call them. They tried to crash

Russell's key group, using—almost strong-arm methods.

'He had to see what was going on. So they all talked in a civilised way, then the two went right on as before. Then Russell spoke to the great man, and he havered and hovered, knowing he was obliged to call them off, but delaying because he was interested in their experiment. Which was sadistic. Morally cruel. Fanatics crop up everywhere.

'Then while Russell and the rest of the team were trying to get him to make a decision, there was a suicide. A girl of about twenty-two. Russell knew her very well, and knew, as they all did, that she'd been hounded to it. *Unwittingly*, he always says, and in the interests of science, but hounded. So the project ended, and the team scattered, and Russell walked away from the only work he was trained to do. So did one of the others. He won't even discuss it.'

The words had fallen on Anna's heart and mind like poison, causing physical pain in her body and head. All this had happened. All this had happened. She knew nothing about it. Almost a stranger.

'I knew some of this,' Stephen said. 'He told me at the beginning of the press. Not the sort of thing you expect to crop up in that atmosphere.'

'It's no secret. There's nothing secret about it. He prefers not to discuss it with me because *I* say: Do something about it. Don't stay out and criticise, you with your superior under-standing.'

'What's the response to that?' Stephen asked, uncon-sciously pulling a face that made his chin longer.

'Oh, well.' Lily stood up. 'There are my cherubs waking up, I think. I gather it's a pretty crass reaction. Being involved, he received some revelation that must remain obscure to me, about the way he ought not to live.'

Stephen said pacifically, 'It is possible.'

'If we're going to be very precious. But I don't like it, and I can think of numerous people—my own family, for instance—who agree with me. It's juvenile behaviour in someone like him.' Mechanically, she gathered the three empty glasses onto the tray. 'But I'm not proud of myself this morning, either. We'd said a few words on the subject before he went out, that's why I've been so vocal. I'll tell him. Confess. Weaken my position.' She smiled wryly. 'I must go to those poor children. Not that there's much wrong with them from the uproar.'

'And we've got to get back to Zo. She wanted to get rid of us with that pudding so that she could concoct some surprise. She's capable of having the house painted purple.'

Lily looked with approval at her brother-in-law as he stood at the top of the steps in the sun, actually showing his teeth in a smile at the prospect of returning to Zoe. She said, 'I can see what Zo means about that anarchist look of yours. It's only partly the hair. You're handsomer these days.'

There was an increase in the clamour from the children's room upstairs. 'I'd better give up. See you soon.' Lily ran inside.

When she and Stephen arrived at the beach, Anna took off her sandals and walked on the sand in her bare feet. 'I suppose she meant all that,' she said, with the slight but habitual feeling of risk that addressing Stephen involved.

He gave a dry laugh. 'She had to, to talk to a non-union member like you.'

'Oh, the family!' They looked at each other and laughed. 'I always knew she regarded me as an outsider, but I was a bit crushed to have it so explicit.'

'Wait till Zo hears.'

They wove round the rock-like bodies lying in the sun.

'Look at the gulls!' Stephen pointed to a slope of sand going down to the water's edge that was used as a runway by the birds. Over and over, they watched the amateurish waddle transmuted to purest curves of flight.

From the other end of the beach, Zoe came to meet them. A few strangers turned to watch her as though a mesmerising hand had touched them. A special person and not for them.

While they tramped across the sand, Stephen told her what they had heard from Lily.

'Then I was all wrong.' Zoe looked up at him with big eyes. 'I thought she'd put pressure on Russell to come back because of her family. What?' She intercepted a glance between the others.

'Yes, she *did*, even before the project shattered, but expecting him to become a leading light out here. Of the right sort. His career was important to Lily.' Stephen tightened his grip round her waist and she leaned against him.

'What was that joke about Lily's family?' She swung forward a little to see Anna, who walked on Stephen's left side. Told, she gave great 'Oh, oh, oh's of indignation.

Anna concluded, 'It's as if only the assurance of relationships laid down by blood and the law prevents her from being quite alone. Our family against all strangers. Close ranks, put up the barricades. She hardly knows what you're like as individuals, only that you're her family. This gives you a kind of otherworldly glamour. She's in love with an idea.'

Hearing all this, Zoe looked solemn and impressed. Half-enquiringly, she said, 'You've given it a lot of thought.'

Stephen squeezed her waist again. 'Anna's aggrieved, aren't you? Because you can't mean you think we have any faults.'

Zoe laughed. 'Oh, no! But, in a way, isn't it natural enough if she prefers her own family? No, it's a bit infatuated. My mother was devoted to us, but less fervid.'

'Well, it may be *natural*—' Anna delivered this with emphasis. 'It's only that it seems strange to me. If you know that but for the relationship you wouldn't exist for someone, it seems—odd. You're not known. Lily says she couldn't imagine having a friend who wasn't related to her. It looks like an inbuilt absence of discrimination, a missing instinct, as if she doesn't know what she likes in people, what really pleases her.'

Her listeners accepted this in silence, with raised brows. Why did Anna mind so much? Kicking up the sand as she walked along, Zoe watched it spume out ahead.

'Anna's right, really. Russell and Lily are very different from each other. I hope it works out. The well-known attraction of opposites. Like us.'

Only yesterday Zoe had been writing in that letter to Joseph about how much alike she and Stephen were. Now they represented the attraction of opposites! Stopping to pick up a small pink shell, Anna noted the contradiction.

'Yes, it's true,' Zoe was saying stoutly. 'All of Lily's attachments are fortuitous. Like a morality play, except that instead of wearing the masks of virtues and vices, you're anonymous behind Daughter, Mother, Father and so on. Anyone might be behind the mask. It would make no difference. The name and the mask tell people how they *ought* to feel, and behave. Outside this framework—chaos. If there's no natural instinct for—'

'Loving,' Anna said.

'Exactly.'

Stephen said, 'Poor Lily,' and opened the garden gate and they trooped through.

'Trip me up, someone.' Anna gave her head a thump with her wrist. 'I have a prejudice against closed systems. Nobody knows how orphans watch families, and nobody knows how an orphan as audience can stimulate family feeling.'

'Except other orphans, presumably,' Stephen said. Then turning to Zoe, he added, 'And Zo knows. Zoe knows everything.'

•

'I wish,' Stephen slashed at his breakfast egg, 'these fools would stop asking you what you're going to do with yourself.'

Startled, Zoe glanced up from unwrapping the morning paper. 'Who? Oh, John! Yes, it is tactless.'

'Tactless?'

'*Stupid*. But they're only making conversation. It doesn't mean anything.'

He tackled his egg again. 'All that pretentious technical stuff about films.'

'That was just because Anna told him I knew Joseph.' Zoe put the paper aside and buttered a slice of toast.

'Why doesn't he ask Anna what she's going to do?'

Anna worked now, since David's death, in a small gallery. She sat at a desk. Occasionally, someone wandered in to look at the paintings. It was often quiet. She read or wrote letters when the place was deserted.

Zoe agreed. 'Well, yes! A widow. Sometimes she still looks about fifteen. I only saw them for those few days in Paris, on their honeymoon. What a shame that had to happen! But she can't spend the next forty years mourning him and sitting in that place.'

'She'll probably marry. But I hope not that Trenchard. Calling himself a movie buff.'

Zoe laughed and gave him a sparkling glance. 'He's quite charming, in his way. Like a charming—cream puff,' she concluded, with a flourish of her knife.

'God!'

'Take no notice.' Zoe put a hand on his knee, looked into his eyes. 'Darling. Take no notice. What he says—silly questions—it's nothing to us.'

He believed her as though her eyes' message to his had literally hypnotised him. Reaching out, he stroked her side, then he resumed the conversation in a tone so untroubled that Zoe looked at him with wonder.

'But there aren't any first-rate women directors, are there? Not that I know much about it.' From the beginning, he had been innocently candid about his opinion of the work she had abandoned.

'No, not many. But, anyway, I wasn't one. Only a low-grade assistant around the place.'

'But with Stranger you were heading that way,' he persisted. 'It was in those interviews. He called you his chief assistant. It's what all these enquirers assume.'

'How would they know? He was kidding. I don't encourage them.' She tried not to feel hounded.

'And if a brilliant one did turn up, with all respect, it isn't very likely that she'd rise up *here*, is it?'

'Talk about the national inferiority complex!' But Zoe was listening now with delight. Months ago, she had realised that she was expected to be quite beyond personal vanity in this matter. Once or twice she had been told of some person on the far fringe of her life who was jealous, or attributed unflattering qualities to her; she had only ever listened inattentively. But no one had ever sought her out, and found her out, and held up mirrors to her, as Stephen had. He thought nothing of her so-called skills. Till recently, she had valued them quite highly. Now, when Lily said, 'That sort of work's all right for someone with no intelligence, but you were wasting yourself,' she had not even demurred. Though somewhere, far off, she saluted the friends of other days.

It was funny to think of it. It seemed quaint that she had

ever wanted to be quite exceptionally good at her chosen work, that for so trivial a purpose her concentration had developed its formidable powers. She had been prepared to work very hard, and had even thought that the work mattered in some more than personal sense. Other people had pandered to this delusion, as she had pandered to theirs—that their life work was of significance.

How clear everything had become since those days! (And yet they were not so far back in time.) And how quickly, without the least desire to deflate or wound, of course, Stephen had dissolved the last of those ideas and ambitions! As if the world could not get along very well without her minute contribution!

Stephen said, 'You don't have to denigrate yourself. But you were only playing around. Painters' and musicians' talents are noticeable while they're children. *You* never intended to be a film director when you grew up.'

She bowed her head over prayerful hands. 'How true! All is as you say. Though you're grinding me into the dust. Sweetheart...'

Ignoring this, Stephen went on argumentatively, 'They all seem to think Stranger's unique in his way, so if you intended to equal him...'

As though it were an instant tonic from which she could expect to draw nimbleness of mind, Zoe took a large bite of toast spread with home-made cherry jam. 'I didn't look at it that way,' she said, somewhat muffled. 'I was interested in the work, not who was equalling whom. You compete with the intractable, not with your fellow toilers. Compete with the difficulty.'

'Oh, well. If you intended to be the best, that's another matter.'

Had she implied that? Zoe scanned his eyes. Often he heard something she hadn't said; often he denied saying what she'd heard. Confusing. 'Have some more coffee.' As she watched the flow from the pot, and moved his cup forward, she said, 'No, I didn't think in that way. *Best.* But when you're quite young, you hope. And you stretch yourself. Make efforts.'

'Ah,' Stephen said, not quite pleasantly exaggerating enlightenment; and she remembered that he had never been young.

'Yes,' she insisted gently. 'But that's all over now, and I'm so glad, so glad. Don't disapprove of the past. I never think about it.' She looked at him with love.

From riding the crest of the wave, from taming tigers, she had turned into this new thing—a suppliant, but a suppliant with a purpose: all to be well with Stephen. She had fallen through him into the universe, into her real self. Yet he was only free spasmodically, as though secret gaolers had him secretly imprisoned somewhere, releasing and confining and tormenting according to some erratic timetable of their own.

After a short silence, Stephen persisted, 'I've never been able to regard the cinema as an art form.' He half-smiled at her, and their eyes held for an instant.

She entreated, 'Please leave it.' In an entirely different tone, two seconds later, gay, light-hearted, Zoe exclaimed, 'Well, frequently it isn't! And I shall cast a fearful spell over Anna's John Trenchard and all movie buffs in a minute, calling on both cats to help.'

Satisfied, he said, 'You know it's rubbish too. Does Anna like him?'

'Moderately, I think. Mainly because he and David were friends. He's some sort of administrator at the Conservatorium,' she said. 'He should be a professional humorist—asking me what I'm going to do for an occupation. There's only *you, you, you*—as the song says. And us, and our harbourside estate, and our cats, and that room full of stuff to be translated, and your printery, and our public life—provided by Russell, and our private life—provided by us...'

As she continued, adding more and more extravagant items to the list, blazing on him, winning him from his invisible oppressors, she was so invested with force that a boundary was crossed. Objects had long dissolved and fallen away. Now, neither of them smiled. They were standing, tightly enlaced; they were sinking together, equally lost.

•

When nothing intervened, Russell drove Anna to and from work. The printery and the gallery were in the same fashionably decrepit area near the docks.

This habit started when she returned from a skiing holiday with a sprained ankle. Zoe said, 'Stephen's gone to Melbourne for a conference, but Russell can collect and deliver you. He'd be glad to.' Zoe could not realise how almost comical, how almost very said, it was, that a third person should feel free to tell Anna anything about him. Even now, while hundreds of facts about their lives had never been exchanged, there was some way in which they knew each other so absolutely that facts were irrelevant, another person's opinion of either a sort of arrogance, a rash effrontery.

Both had a capacity for deep and lasting friendship; neither saw why the other sex should be excluded because of property rights. Admittedly, affectionate regard, admiration, the discerning appreciation of another's qualities were, for certain persons, volatile agents. But they had lived their particular lives. Their characters had formed a long time ago. There was no danger. For ages now, long after Anna's ankle was forgotten, Russell had continued to drive her home at night when they both happened to be free. Lily had no objection: she was accustomed to his having multitudinous commitments; this was one among many.

In the beginning, there was innocent hilarity, raillery, an air of delight that her sprained ankle had resulted in this luck, this time spent travelling to and fro which was, somehow, so great a relief to them both. Their pleasure was perfectly harmless. Russell had known her, after all, since she was fifteen! Because of their recognition of each other, they had always fallen into close, familiar conversation when they were alone. With the confidence of those who know themselves well and feel the issues of their lives decided, quite without misgivings (they were not likely to underestimate what was owing to others), they had allowed themselves to enjoy the extraordinary ease of being together.

Gradually, something had gone wrong. They were like travellers in the Himalayas. Immensity, the momentous, surrounded them inescapably. They laughed too much; they talked too quickly, and too obviously at random. The silent immensity would not go away. Since they knew so exactly what was permissible, and were so scrupulous, they were dismayed by these changes, and could only begin to place heavier and heavier guards on their behaviour. Previously, their common awareness that they could not misunderstand each other made circumspection unnecessary. Now, it seemed that that very impossibility which had been the basis of the light-heartedness, the freedom spun between them, was what made watchfulness so essential.

Tonight, held up at a red light, Russell turned to her. 'Is the exhibition sold out?'

'You saw it.'

'Yes. He's going through a bad time. The four in the corner are best.'

She nodded emphatically, then looked ahead at the road.

He went on, 'Zo and Stephen were marrying you off to John Trenchard.'

Anna said nothing. Then she said, 'Oh, were they!' and meticulously scanned the traffic-jammed road ahead, and the buildings on either side of the street. 'No, of course not,' she said in a low hurried tone. 'How could they think so?'

Glancing into her eyes, then back at the road, Russell said,

'Oh, it happens often enough. There's a wedding party now.' A long black car full of white tulle and flowers passed.

'It happens. No, we don't even go out any more.'

In the years since David's death, several agreeable men of between thirty and forty-five had gravitated towards Anna—the divorced, the bachelors, the deserted husbands. She went out with them and listened. Their problems had for the time being resolved themselves into one: the lack of a wife, a proper home life. Odd men out, unclaimed, they wanted to be found. Their manner declared it from the start, and within days or weeks, it was stated unequivocally.

By remaining silent, Russell gave the impression of requiring a further explanation. Casting a glance at his profile, Anna cleared her throat.

'He wants to marry someone. You can't let people waste their time and money if you're not going to take them seriously. There are plenty of women who'd think themselves lucky to get him. He's lonely. I suppose a lot of people are lonely. Then, almost anyone who strikes them as—*quite nice*—will do. It doesn't have to be a particular person, or even a certain sort of person.'

Speaking in a tone of enormous objectivity, looking straight ahead, Anna felt her skeleton waver secretly, as though it were seaweed pressed about by movements of deepest seas, invisible on the glittering surface.

'Not everybody differentiates between people as much as you do.' Russell's voice was somehow careful.

'Aren't they lucky!'

'No.'

She gave a brief, sad smile. 'They show a lot of sense.'

'No.'

This sombre, monosyllabic Russell alarmed her. She rushed on, 'Of course, if you want more and don't get it, you miss more. But even that might be better than wanting less in the first place.'

'We all like what we want.'

There was a conscious silence.

Winding the car window up and then down again, Anna said hastily, 'So if *their* being quite nice isn't enough, you have to undeceive people. I can't see the world as a great hospital with us all nursing and pitying each other. There's something better than that. What I mean is—I never pity anyone I care for, so if what someone wants is pity, I can't care for him.'

They halted at a traffic light. An unaccompanied labrador wearing a studded collar walked over the pedestrian crossing in front of six lanes of cars reined in at the starting barrier.

The lights changed. On both sides of the median strip the traffic surged forward. Russell said, 'You've had your share of neurotics. But I always feel sorry for people. What have you got against it?'

Out of dark experience, not expecting understanding even from him, she said, understating, 'I've seen it do a lot of harm. One person pitied at bitter cost to someone else, with the well-meaning pitier unaware of all except his good intentions.'

'Are you thinking of your uncle?'

'Not only him. He was only one sort of pitier—blinded by a single obsession and murdered by it. Complex, truthful, feeling people give me great joy. Pitiable people give others great joy. (Charles wasn't like that.) And in both cases, the more complex and so on, and the more pitiable, the better.'

'You like to appreciate; they like to help and be charitable.'

'Ah, yes. But to satisfy their yearnings, someone has to be in an inferior position. The holy satisfaction of having done good to the weak is one I'm wary of.'

'You wouldn't see them abandoned. I'm almost certain you'd give a steak to a starving man.'

She smiled. 'But dispassionately. No, with someone like Charles it's the maniacal exclusiveness of his pity; in the others, it's the assumption of the mantle of one abler and wiser that I feel as corrupting.'

'Why? They might be.' He looked along his shoulder at her.

'Because I've had my life incidentally broken by the pity directed at the deserving; because I've maniacally pitied and know the holy satisfaction; because I've been abler and wiser and corrupted.'

'In these few years?'

She smiled again with closed lips. 'I started young.'

'Corrupt and complex as you are, I appreciate you.' The humour had gone from his voice long before he finished speaking.

Almost inaudibly, she said, 'Oh, don't.'

They listened painfully to their last remarks.

Anna said, 'I've seen good people bleed themselves to death from pity. I've seen the pitied splash in their life's blood, like children playing with water.'

'In other words,' Russell said, 'you sometimes feel a deep pity for those who pity, and sometimes for the pitied, everything depending on the individual and the circumstance.'

After a second, she said, 'Yes. So you seem to have proved.'

'Where have you seen this?'

'Here and there.'

In a less than natural voice, Russell went on, 'No, in public we need more justice than the country thinks it can afford, and in private something more equal—like love.'

They both smiled perfunctorily in the hope of turning this into an ordinary conversation. Russell's hands on the steering wheel were brown, fine-boned. With him, Anna felt alive, real, relaxed, stimulated, at home, happy. She had genuinely liked a number of men she had known in recent years, and felt a genuine sympathy. But she could not fail to see that, against her will, the company of the withdrawn, the melancholic, the hysterical had begun to repel her.

Having found a bus ticket in her pocket, she now pleated, folded and re-pleated it as she spoke. 'Even Stephen fills me with a frightful feeling of resistance when he's temperamental. (Though he's changed so much with Zo.) But sooner or later people have to take up their own lives, not disperse them out as though they were knitting wool that a clever knitter might handle better.' She paused in her important ticket folding. 'Everyone who wants help can't come first in your life, because they'd have to remain first. And then, you'd have to become promiscuous at every level of existence to please everyone.'

'Oh, Anna, Anna!' Russell turned out of the traffic down a side street. And they glanced simultaneously at each other, and exchanged in the split second during which their eyes met, a long uneasy look.

Her thoughts seemed to climb a steep staircase. They had frightened each other today, she and Russell. If someone said, 'Boo!' through the car windows, they would both have heart attacks. What they had just indicated to each other—that there was nothing to be done—was not new. But it felt new. Anna thought: it's necessary. It's quite right. I think I can bear it.

Quickly they drove on, leaving the look behind. Russell was with her; she was brilliantly happy.

'You can't stay locked up with those paintings forever,' he said.

'No. I'll do something. There are so many things I should learn. Even at this advanced age, I ought to do something brain stretching.'

'Ought. Ought.'

Looking straight ahead, they were both smiling. They started to talk again, glancing with admiration and curiosity at the shabby views of shops and apartment buildings: they might have been watching dolphins play. Russell told her about the press and, as always, startled her and made her laugh aloud. He was an inspired mimic.

When they stopped at her flat, Anna said rapidly, 'That

was good of you, Russell. I can't ask you in. I'm going out to dinner.'

'Ah. You don't warn everybody off, then?' He watched intently.

'Not instantly. I'm no recluse. The timing's important. Russell—for a few days I'll be staying late at the gallery. I'll catch a bus. I know you're busy too.'

After a pause, he said, 'I'll ring you,' and was gone.

Anna shut the front door and went through the flat to the bedroom. Shoes off, bag and newspaper dropped beside them, she lay on the bed. After all those years separated—postcards, a few letters, snatches of news from letters to other people, now, quite often, quite often... The sun had jumped from the sky and taken up residence in her. She felt light stream from her hair and eyes, from the tips of her fingers. It would be all right. It was all for something. *Obviously*. It had to be.

Russell. Lying on her bed, Anna let memories, always ready to swamp and overwhelm her, take over. About themselves, their situation, they both knew everything. Words were redundant. All that was needed was very great care. Anna sucked in her upper lip and held it between her teeth. It provided, temporarily, some sort of balance for her mind, this soft lip firmly held. To hold the balance, to be able to bear her life without Russell, not to fall into despair, would require extreme carefulness, constant caution. Silently, with the conscious effort of one scaling mountains, she breathed in, filling her lungs. In obedience to nothing deliberately thought, her mind moved on, shifting those only just bearable pictures.

That's right. She was so lucky, so lucky when you looked at it in the right way. Russell. Russell's absence. Then there was David, who could be married because it was what he wanted, and nothing mattered. Well, she liked to please and he had been pleased and mattered more than she expected. But it was too late. He appeared too late ever to seem much more than a kind second-best. 'I'm sorry. Nobody's fault,' she whispered aloud. A pity. But nobody's fault. It was only that she knew what she liked. She liked Russell.

A sudden screeching of traffic outside, downstairs, woke her to the present. Dragging herself up like a swimmer drugged with saltwater and air from a pool, she tried to concentrate on the night ahead, and shook her head to shake Russell out of it. She jumped over a low stool and started to pull off her clothes for the shower. Alive and still young and hopeful, after all. So happy. It was enough that he existed.

While she was having a shower, the telephone rang. She ran to it, grabbing a towel, leaving wet footprints on the way.

Zoe said with a kind of determined calm, 'Anna. Did Stephen leave a silver pencil when we were over the other night?'

'I don't think so. It isn't the one that belonged to my father? To our father?' (She never know how to refer to the parents who died without leaving memories.) With her free hand, Anna wrapped the towel round herself and sat on the arm of the easy chair.

'Exactly.' There was a hard silence from Zoe, then she said in a hard voice, 'You knew about it? I thought it was just a silver pencil. He suspected someone from work had stolen it, or that Mrs Trent might have taken a fancy to it. To begin with I didn't even know what was wrong, only that something cataclysmic had happened.'

'Well, the pencil,' Anna said, feeling the hopelessness of trying to describe its importance in Stephen's scheme of things. 'It was all he had belonging to them. Charles got rid of everything.'

In a strained voice, Zoe said, 'I've always been so stifled by family possessions that it wouldn't matter to me if they disintegrated this minute.'

Anna said nothing, found an end of the towel and dabbed at her face, feeling her heart beat with consternation.

'It's been gone for three days. He wouldn't say what was wrong. Then I was told about the pencil, but not that it had any special...Being helpful, I unfortunately bought him a new one.'

'Oh!'

'Yes, oh!'

'I'll search around. It might have fallen down the side of a chair.' But she understood from Zoe's voice that the restoration of the hallowed object would in no way atone for its disappearance.

Anna returned to the shower, cold and shivering. She dressed and applied make-up carefully to her face. For a time, she did think of Stephen and Zoe. Then she found herself back in the sitting room with blessed minutes to spare before Andrew was due to arrive. All of her, her spirit, went to Russell as though he were her home. As if a voice had called as she was closing a door, she heard and considered with a sort of numb disquiet, the question: *What are you going to do?* Initiative and efforts were expected because she was alone. People did like you to appear to have some purpose in life.

Back from four months in Europe after the wedding, settled into David's flat crammed with paintings, records, books, the question was asked seriously for the first time. David said, prophetically, 'If I died young, what would happen to you? Apart from another husband.'

'Why would you do a thing like that? Ghoul! (That's the first time I've ever said "ghoul".)'

And then, it seemed in retrospect, events tumbling over one another—David less than well, David consulting the local doctor and perhaps seeming better for days and then definitely worse; then specialists, hospital, treatment, twice-daily visits, the first thoughts of danger. Straws in the wind, they said, and the first thoughts were just like that. Then there were giant steps taken moment by moment, steadily, into the heart of an enormous phantasmagoria. David, doctors, nurses, friends. Then there was nothing. It was all over and she was left in that enormous space. Life was a dream. People were smoke. Day-to-day events were unreal. Time and pretence went on.

Then everyone came home from Europe, and Stephen from Melbourne, and more time sped past. She and Russell saw each other frequently, in crowded situations. But now...At the beginning of the year, probably, she would take hold of her life again. Obviously she couldn't lie on her bed thinking about him forever.

The résumé of well-known events flashed through Anna's mind like a falling star, and with the same inevitability, her mind plunged back to him.

When the metallic hammering of the door knocker sounded in the flat, Anna started slightly with shock, and a tiny chill went out from her heart to her skin, and her spirit reluctantly closed down. Andrew. How unfair to everyone that the knowing of one person, the separation, should so poison and diminish every other association. She thought: I mustn't let it. I must try.

PART THREE

'It was mean of Zo not to take any pictures of the girls.' Lily's daughters had been awarded ballet scholarships and were on the point of leaving for London. Since the announcement, the house had been spring-cleaned twice with Lily, who never did housework, working like a demon beside Mrs Glad. She was up at daybreak. Now she was tidying the linen cupboard, building towers of white and coloured oblongs.

Passing her, Russell was offered this criticism of his sister. 'It's been a long time since she's touched a camera.'

'So she said. But she could hardly have forgotten how.'

'People lose their confidence. It's years since she's handled one.'

'Confidence!' Lily doubled a folded sheet with a blow from the side of her hand. 'She's never lacked that. You heard Stephen. He agreed with me. He said professionals were too snobbish to take pictures of relations.'

Russell scraped at a callous on the palm of his hand. That a fineness of intelligence in one area could be allied with emotional or moral insanity in others was proved, he felt, more often than necessary. Lily, now fiercely tidying the cupboard because of the girls' imminent departure, had never noticed in all these years that Zoe was no longer a confident person. And other things.

He said, 'Yes, I heard him. I heard you talking to her while I was getting the drinks. She *was* ill,' he pointed out. 'She *was* in hospital with pneumonia a few hours later.'

Over her shoulder, clasping a pile of sheets to her breast, Lily gave him a malign look and said nothing.

'Roy took photographs. I thought you liked them.'

'You always defend her. Zo's champion. If Stephen's jealous, no one could blame him.' Abruptly, she stuffed the linen into the cupboard. Keeping her back turned to him, she said, 'No need to stand watching me. I'm capable of managing without supervision.'

In the bathroom, Russell started to shave.

Lily had convinced herself that her daughters should be doctors. Medicine enthralled her. What worthier career existed? Ballet was only for posture, a pastime. To the surprise of no one but Lily, having practised to the point of martyrdom, proved their excellence, won coveted awards and the praise of persons competent to praise, Caroline and Vanessa were leaving home and country. Now that she was forced to hear, Lily was outraged and grieved as though their plans had been secret. She endured the breaking-in of this fended-off truth, as people must, as though it were a serious illness and, like an illness, it was locked in her, impossible to share. She denied its existence. It could not be mentioned. She thought of nothing else.

In other days, Lily's talent for misjudging other persons' natures had culminated in her belief that Russell was attached to Ilsa Prescott, the local doctor's wife. Understanding that a sound judgment of her fellows was not one of Lily's strengths, Russell was startled nonetheless that she could think him susceptible to Ilsa Prescott's acid attractions. Like everyone, he was still learning.

Hearing of Lily's innuendoes, Zoe had laughed. 'Ilsa's a decorative cookie, but you'd shatter a tooth if you took a bite. What's wrong with Lily's head? You haven't got time to lead anything but a blameless life. And if you led the other sort with Ilsa, I'd wonder what was wrong with *your* head.'

'Give Lily a break, there's a good girl.'

'You were the one to complain about being misjudged.'

Russell hissed air through clenched teeth. 'My feeble attempt at light humour. Idle chat.'

'But how could she?'

'Seemed quite easy. I know you think Lily's no judge of character. But it isn't the only capacity worth anything in life.'

But Zoe looked down dully. 'She's not alone in that. But it is the only capacity worth anything.' Almost desperately, she looked up. 'It is. It is. It's sanity. It's being sane. There may be better things than seeing dead straight, but not many from where I stand. Because if you don't, you're dangerous.'

'Or in danger, or both.'

After a pause, Zoe changed the subject. 'Did I stop you from going for a walk with Anna? It didn't matter, did it?'

'Not a bit.'

'After all, your mother-in-law had voted herself into the party, too.'

'She's a good egg, Lily senior. All her wits about her.'

Russell shaved, showered and dressed. As he felt for the car keys, he remembered that he and Zoe were cleaning fish, leaning over a rock pool cleaning fish, while they talked. He had lifted a silvery bream by the tail.

Lily had organised one of her regular family gatherings; a holiday weekend, and fifteen assorted individuals were assembled in the house belonging to her mother near the deserted Ten Mile Beach on the south coast. Lily was preparing lunch. The girls were practising. He and Anna were going for a walk, but Zoe conspicuously claimed him as a fishing partner, so Anna and Stephen went for a walk with Lily's mother. It was grey, unseasonably cool; the air smelled of rain. Zoe had fished beside him on the rocks at one end of the empty beach, totally silent. Thinking of Anna, he remembered Lily's extraordinary insinuations about Ilsa Prescott, and mentioned her. Zoe became almost animated, as though she felt it a relief to think of something to say.

'All right if we take the car?' Vanessa caught him as he came out into the hall. 'We'll drop you off at work. We're not all that popular in other directions, if you know what I mean, so we'd better have yours.'

'Don't worry about your popularity.' He put an arm round

this straight-backed, frail-looking steely girl who was his daughter. For a moment Russell looked into her face. She and Caroline were beautiful girls, with high foreheads, rounded chins, large eyes, straight noses, long dark hair, and expressions that accurately pointed to dispositions intelligent, gay and unyielding.

'You can have the car, but talk to your mother. She'll come round.'

'She'd better. We'll be gone in three days.' Deep elation replaced the momentary qualm.

'You couldn't manage to look forlorn when your mother's in your vicinity? Not that I'd want you to perjure yourself!'

'God forbid!' She gave him an enraptured look. 'Not possibly.'

'Quite right! I have a daughter who's no hypocrite.'

'Don't tease. Are you ready? Caroline's in the car.'

They went downstairs together. Vanessa admired her father's shirt and told him its blue exactly matched his eyes.

'Such a command of flattery!' Russell said. 'I'll never know why your mother thinks you're helpless.'

'She has to protect us. She can go back to lecturing and protect hordes of students now. She'll like that. We've never been dependent enough.'

Russell listened in silence to this just appraisal. 'Have you both said goodbye?...Then wait for me in the car.'

He went off to find Lily, who seemed to have abandoned the linen cupboard halfway through. The girls waited. He would not be able to see Anna. She had been home for four months after a year in Canada. He had scarcely seen her since the exhibition of her work at the gallery near the press.

'I still wonder,' Lily turned from the beautiful pottery with admiration, 'what there was left for Canada to teach you. And why Canada?'

'Much it had to teach me. A master potter lives there.' Harder, more assured, Anna stood with her friends.

'If the master contributed to this, it was worth it!' Lily generously declared.

'Thank you, Lily! But it was no penance.' With the air of one choosing at last to tell the truth, Anna said, 'I went really because the mountains are high, and the snow is white.'

Since then, every attempt to meet was frustrated by her work or his work, appointments, business, duties. He had no idea how much, or if, she minded. Even the walk in the country…And now another day would go by during which they would not meet.

•

Zoe sometimes thought of those laboratory animals that were the subjects of experiments. They were deliberately confused beyond the capacity of their powers of adjustment. Finally they lay in the bottom of the cage, taking no notice any more of the captors, the coaxing and cajolery that would persuade them to embark again on the routine torment. Political prisoners were often destroyed in the same way, on purpose; and vain people like me, Zoe thought, who think they can adjust and adjust indefinitely to another person's irrationality, in the mysterious hope of pleasing and somehow making well that same irrationality. Like Stephen's Uncle Charles with his wife, Nicole. Like a lot of people.

•

Be satisfied. Be satisfied. This is what you wanted. This is what you've got.

Addressing Stephen, who was some miles off, on his way home from work, Zoe touched the cutlery on the table, eyed the stark flower arrangements put about by Mrs Trent for the convalescent's first dinner sitting up, out of bed, for weeks.

Be satisfied. The injunction came from her heart, as though it literally had a voice.

In the course of carrying in hot drinks these days since Zoe had been out of hospital, Mrs Trent had told her of three women who were consulting a hypnotist for relief from ailments and miseries. Zoe let her imagination play over the idea as though it were a possibility. She would ask him to remove *Be satisfied* from her mind. She would say, 'I have the impression that I died two or three years ago, and I don't know what to do about it.' So what did she want? Just to be resurrected.

Disguising his merriment and contempt, he would put his fingertips together. 'My good lady, a very simple matter. Easily mended.' He would write on a card, like a doctor, 'Dead, but won't lie down.'

'But I'm the guilty party,' she would tell him. 'I let it happen. Let the words be said, and listened. Agreed to be devalued to the point where I'm of less consequence than anyone in the world. Permanently in the wrong.'

The hypnotist would nod sagely.

Wandering about this room, once so pleasing to her in its lack of fashionable starkness at one extreme, and of fashionable clutter at the other, she caught sight of her reflection in the french windows. Forty. *Forty*. So many years, leading to this disaster that could be told to no one.

When Stephen came in, Zoe was pulling the plastic bags from some dry-cleaning delivered earlier in the afternoon.

He said, 'You're not supposed to be up. Why are you doing that?'

She lifted her face to be kissed, but he averted his head so that her lips touched his cheek. As always now, she had the sensation, when their eyes met, of sustaining a physical injury. A speechless, difficult resentment went out from them both. Frequently, like very tall people conversing over the heads of a crowd, they spoke across their grievances about the local scene, the world situation, the arts. There was a time when this had been safe, but now there was danger everywhere. These conversations were farcical. What was a fine point of principle to her any more? His principles were weapons used to beat her down. So high-minded about the distant injustices of the world! Men were marvellous. Perhaps it was marvellous to rise above the personal. There was a story about to that effect. She had never believed it, told by influential persuaders though it was.

She said, 'The doctor thinks I should start getting up soon. Did you have any word today about the contract?'

'We've got it. We're printing the whole series.' He was impassive, weary.

'What are they—history texts?'

Sliding his coat off, Stephen loosened his tie. 'History, then maths. We'll have more work than we can handle.'

'Are you pleased?' With closed lips she smiled in appeal, wishing him hope and encouragement.

'I suppose so. Russell's pleased,' he said pointedly, meeting her eyes with a curious boldness.

Assuming indifference, Zoe turned away. Long ago, she had ceased to mention Russell's name. 'Would you like a drink? Or do you want a shower before dinner?'

Nervousness, enmity, went out from both of them. They were like spies working for hostile governments. The game was up; all was known, but nothing had been said out loud. They continued to do their little calculations, carefully adding and subtracting, laying false trails, collecting evidence for their reports.

'I'll just have a wash. I'll have something to drink with dinner.' Coat in one hand, briefcase in the other, he went upstairs.

Zoe pressed the soft plastic bags in her hands into a ball.

At dinner, Stephen suddenly put down his glass. 'Your hair. It's not right for your face like that.'

'Oh, you don't think so?'

'It's too old, or young. Doesn't suit you.' He seemed to be

under the impression that her hair was irritating him dreadfully.

'Easy.' With the removal of a few invisible clips it fell, dark and shining, into the shape it had had last week before Stephen had desired a change in that arrangement. Zoe forbore to mention this. She knew well enough what her crime was. She could see him trying to feel appeased. Since he was not in close touch with himself, he might even for a moment have succeeded. He had asserted himself; she had submitted.

Mysteriously, he seemed not to notice that they ran through this sort of performance quite regularly. Any excuse served for criticism: the way she spoke on the telephone, the way she cut the bread, the shrubs she ordered from the nursery, the books she chose to read, any belief, feeling or action. He could not be pleased. Quite often it was some idle statement, some lightly held opinion, that he pounced on with a ferocity out of all proportion to the depth of her involvement.

There were times when she felt like someone who had chosen to pander to the whims of a despotic interior decorator. The propriety of taking part in the performance struck her as dubious. Minds operate on so many levels at once: there was a limit beyond which he might not go without destroying her feelings for him. Since she had somehow placed her life in him, the danger was great indeed. He approached her at night, but the essential grievance, he himself, remained under lock and key. She might have been a handsome woman whose geography he had grown used to in a brothel.

Across the table she glanced at him. Where had he gone,

that lover, that loved one? She sat with Stephen's effigy. He was the tomb of them both. Like a wraith, she visited the stone images. Eating, they continued to skirmish, silently sustaining thorny scratches, haemorrhages, and blows of extreme subtlety and variety. Last night—reconciliation, now these calculating looks, and in each chest Zoe saw the grinding stones turn again, and the sharpening-up proceed. The stakes were so high, although occasionally they both forgot what they were, as generals in the midst of battles must have trouble recalling the philosophy on which the carnage rests.

'What are you going to do now?' he asked, when dinner ended. 'Leave the dishes for Mrs Trent. You should go back to bed.'

Touched by his concern, Zoe agreed almost timidly, 'Perhaps I'd better.'

Elaborately casual, Stephen asked, 'Who do you suppose does the dishes for Mrs Trent when she's ill?'

'I should think her husband or her daughter.'

He gave a small, foolish smile. 'I hadn't thought of that. Zo...' Now that he had lost the round and she seemed cold, he searched for a reason to delay her. 'Anna's coming over this week, you said?'

'Yes.' She pulled the sash of her dressing gown tighter round her waist.

'See how she is. There could be something wrong.'

From habit, Zoe wondered what he meant, apart from what he said. She saw that he wanted to establish contact now, having broken it, and was willing to throw Anna in as an offering. Zoe had tossed him many a morsel of this kind with reckless shame.

'I don't seem to be getting much of a response to my no-doubt boring remarks.'

'I was waiting for you to go on.' The conversation had a quite peculiar familiarity to Zoe. Usually, *she* struggled to rouse life and interest in Stephen with the very same words. Now it had all turned dizzily round. A sensation of the circularity of things came to her. She marvelled at the efforts, the responsibilities, at the memory of what had been destroyed. What a pity that this, all the time, was what he had wanted!

'Why do you think there's something wrong with Anna?' she asked, playing straight man.

'That weekend at Ten Mile Beach just after she came home. We all went in different directions that Sunday morning. Mary and Ian went to church, and Lily was getting lunch. You insisted Russell had to go fishing with you, and Anna and I went for a walk with Mrs Irving.'

'Yes. It was a lovely morning, then it rained, and everyone enjoyed our fish.'

Stephen nodded. 'It started to rain while we were out, so Lily's mother decided to go back and help with lunch. I took her to the path near the house, and Anna went on by herself. I was looking for her for about ten minutes, and got myself stuck in a thick patch of thorny stuff. Then I pushed through to the edge of a clearing—'

'Well, what happened?' Zoe asked awkwardly, infected by his sudden awkwardness.

'She didn't know I was there. She was in a bad way.'

Over their empty cups and glasses, they exchanged dismayed looks.

'What?...Crying?'

He nodded and offered her a cigarette. 'She was sitting on a big fallen tree. I went away.'

'I've never known Anna to cry. No, thanks. Against orders.'

'That's right. You're not allowed to.' Lighting one for himself, holding it in his mouth for a moment, Stephen shut the packet.

'Well. That's horrible.' Zoe looked at him, confused. 'You couldn't have gone over to her?'

He shook his head.

Zoe checked an impulse to speak. Once so impulsive, she was now very, very skilled at checking impulses.

'I went home to the house. She came in about three-quarters of an hour later. She'd been caught in the storm. She called through the kitchen window to Lily that she was going to dry her hair and change her clothes.'

'She doesn't know you saw her?'

'No. When she came out of her room, I thought the other must have been a mirage. Because if someone had died...'

Despair. Zoe shook her head, realising that she could think of no one whose death, supposing anyone had died, would cause Anna such overwhelming grief. Yet someone had that power. More and more she could remember the weekend. Highly disagreeable it had been. Lily's fierce and alarming reaction to her daughters' scholarships showed itself for the first time. Mrs Irving took Zoe aside, and explained that it was Lily's age that was affecting her so. The girls objected to being called monsters of selfishness, and said that that sort of abuse and attitude were dated. Placated by their father, they devoted the remainder of the short holiday to practice. Nothing broke their discipline. Everyone kept disappearing stealthily and returning to an apprehensive circle of eyes.

'Maybe it's something to do with Tom. He's lingered around for years, though I'd thought with very little encouragement. No. It must be something in Canada, someone there.'

'What do you suggest, then?'

Again Zoe refrained from suggesting that it might have been easier to speak to Anna then, than to approach her with questions now.

'I don't know what to think. Years ago this might have been less amazing. But after she got so involved in her classes, and when she was so good at it...She had the studio for ages. Then Canada was obviously terrific for her. Her work's really something! I thought she was happy. She's changed...There must have been bad years after David died.'

There was no doubt that Anna had had amorous adventures with a number of men. Living alone near the city, disinclined to discuss lovers and friends, she had preserved tracts of private life to herself. Was it possible that sheer persistence, his dogged way of hanging about for years through the arrival and departure of others, had worn Anna down to the point of marrying Tom?

Play the field. Anna liked to play the field. Possibly only Zoe, of all her friends, knew. She had found out by accident, and was curiously shocked because Anna hadn't cared. There had been enigmatic years before this, when heaven only knew what her preoccupations were beyond what was visible. Intent on Stephen, on her own life, on scrawling across blank diary pages the secret words 'Happy days' that she found undecipherable now, Zoe hadn't even wondered. Perhaps there had been some crucial break after which came the casual affairs, with Anna acting like anyone with a taste for sleeping about. She could hardly have been in love with them all. But if not, it seemed out of character.

Now, Zoe pressed her hands down on the table and stood up. 'Anyway. I'm going to bed.'

'Is that all you have to say?'

Lifting some plates, Zoe trailed out to the kitchen, Stephen following. 'I think so.'

She understood, without feeling it, that there was a sadness in her failure to respond. He had tried to interest her by exhibiting Anna; now something was expected in return. It was a quandary. She returned the milk and butter to the fridge, and shook a tin of grapefruit juice to see how much remained. Meanwhile, she rummaged in her mind for some way of amusing and enlivening Stephen. Once upon a time, nothing he said or did could discourage her. Her fiery temper might never have existed. The lively and cajoling woman he sometimes liked and sometimes loathed appeared and disappeared according to his unpredictable preferences or years. Then one day when no one was noticing, she simply failed to come back on demand. They both felt inclined to disbelieve the change in her. But her eyes told him bitterly: you can play games for just so long. This is what you wanted. The enthusiasm that gave him happiness and repelled him no longer existed.

Sliding his arms around her, Stephen waited for her to move. When she merely stood quiet and obedient, head averted, trying to feel in her dressing-gown pocket for a handkerchief, he said, 'You're not very forthcoming.'

Numerous reasonable but inflammatory replies came to mind. Everything was bait. She said with stoic good humour, 'Officially, I'm not out of bed yet. I might do some work for an hour, when I go up.'

'Must you?' He kissed the side of her throat.

'I promised this paper,' she said, seeming apologetic, but experiencing the faint self-satisfaction of a tightrope walker so without fear that she hardly knew how to gauge her own fearlessness.

In a rather formal tone, Stephen said, 'When you're better, see if you can talk to Anna, will you?'

'Of course.' They exchanged a look. And in the three or four seconds of its duration, with shutters flung wide, the blood was, the oxygen was, the flashing colours and violence of their true life.

Lying again in bed, hemmed in by dictionaries and notebooks, Zoe felt a moment's compunction recalling Stephen's insincere request. She was mortified but not surprised to realise how easily they had both forgotten Anna and her astonishing grief, except in so far as her plight could be used to gain some personal advantage.

Drowning men can't be expected to save other drowning men, she assured herself: then she remembered that it was always a potentially drowning man who went to the rescue, and sometimes he was the one to be lost.

•

'You didn't go to the ship?' Zoe asked, glancing up at her sister-in-law. She and Anna were wandering through the garden, chased from the house by the banging of plumbers in the kitchen.

'No, I didn't want to.'

Zoe raised her brows. 'There were stacks of people there, Russell said. It sounded quite gay, in spite of Lily's taking it so hard.'

'It must have been harrowing for her—the streamers, and "Auld Lang Syne" and "Till We Meet Again". They do pile it on. I took Vanessa and Caroline to lunch the other day and said goodbye then.'

Summer again, but a cold wind was blowing up from the South Pole. Zoe felt it go through the thin wool of her jacket. 'The girls showed me the silver bracelets you gave them. They were thrilled.'

Anna gave an almost querulous shake of one hand.

'The most dedicated, one-track-minded girls I've ever come across.'

'Enviably talented.' Anna smiled faintly. 'Sit down, Zo.

They're still using a road drill in your kitchen.' She sat on the low stone wall and Zoe joined her.

'They say their mother is only wounded in her academic ambitions. They've got it all worked out. They giggle away. They're absolutely right, and absolutely heartless, because when the chips were down, all she really wanted was their presence in Sydney.'

'Quite a big all!' Anna commented. 'She wants her way. They want their lives. Everyone's said for years that they'd have to go abroad to dance. I've always understood Lily couldn't wait to get back to work.'

Zoe gave a keening sound. 'It's not as simple as that. They were frail babies. But she hired a nurse and went back to work quite soon after they were born. Then it looked as if they weren't going to live. I think she must have bargained with fate and sworn never to put work before them again. She had every chance of reaching dizzy academic heights, and that was what she wanted.'

A look of scepticism in her eye, Anna listened. 'So what are you saying? That they should have been sorry for her, and sacrificed their chances?'

'Of course not. Children will go away, and they should. I don't disagree with you. I don't know. I haven't given it all that much thought.'

For some seconds the two sat silent, watching the stirring of grass blades, stems and leaves. A cluster of daisies bent before the wind. Since Anna's arrival earlier this morning—relaxed, detached, ready to laugh—Zoe had tried to penetrate her own diffidence in the face of her friend's self-possession. In other days she would have barged straight in, never feeling the invasion of Anna's privacy as a hurdle. Now, try though she would to ask, 'Is anything wrong?' her intention lapsed when she glanced into Anna's eyes. She had forgotten how to muster toughness and self-assertion. Feeling pusillanimous, she referred again to Lily.

'I know she's sometimes too forceful for comfort. Everyone says she's a born teacher, and it carries over into private life. Like having a Test cricketer bat and bowl during dinner.'

'Shop talk's fun if it's your shop. But talents meant for public use are lethal in private.'

'Lily, you mean?'

'All of us.' Anna stared about at the garden. 'Unless you're lucky enough to use them up in the proper work, they run over the edge into family life and'—she paused and said lightly—'muck up everything. The worst thing is, it often takes such a long time to recognise what the chief strength is. You might only deduce it at forty or fifty by looking back on what you've done wrong.' She laughed. 'Think how much less damage I do—moulding and cracking clay instead of people.'

As though the highly selective attention inside her which languished through days and nights that provided no sustenance for its deepest wants—to understand what had happened to her life, to understand natures different from her own—as though this attention had at last been riveted, Zoe said, 'It happened to me, I think. Public talents wrecking private life.

Not,' she added, turning to Anna with a vague inward look, 'that I realised that clearly till this moment. I liked—to make things better, to contribute myself, somehow. Potentially, I was a psychotherapist. A creative worker. I liked to discover things. That's it really. Most of all that disappeared into my work in Paris.'

As she spoke, her mind added that sadly, unkindly, unwisely, destructively, she had given all of this attention, like a ray of too great intensity, to one person, to the general detriment and waste.

I married his neurosis, she thought dispassionately. I was attracted by the strangeness of his mind as a psychiatrist might have been drawn to an interesting case. He wanted a resident analyst. Neither of us understood.

At the time, the facts had scarcely presented themselves in this light. Having fallen from the feather bed of her life at home into other feather beds in Paris, it happened that she had only read about but never met a real neurotic. But what *she* failed to recognise in Stephen, her instinct did.

Anna nodded, recognising Zoe's description of herself, and the correctness of the past tense.

Hastily, with an unreal laugh, Zoe went on, 'Let's blame my doting parents and be in fashion. Nothing was expected of me except that I should please myself. I can see now that I needed and yearned for a person and a task that would make extreme demands so that I could know who I was. But there were no pressures. A few examinations were made much of. I was praised till self and wants came out of my ears. The self-dramatising amused the family and they encouraged it. Self-indulgence on their part.'

'Yes, I thought that.'

'Did you notice?'

'Of course. This stone's getting hard, Zo. What about going up on to the verandah? No, at first you seemed tremendously lucky. You were so treasured. You could do absolutely no wrong.'

'Oh, I was an idol.'

They climbed the steps and sat down. Several books lay on the floor near Zoe's chair. Inside, the plumbers were shouting above the sound of their transistor as they replaced some copper piping.

'Later, when I'd got over envy and admiration enough to focus straight, I thought they were rather cruel to you. Because I was younger, but knew so much more about what I used to call "real life" and people.'

'Retarded by prosperity and love. They had to keep their little girl.'

'I'm not recommending *my* experience as the ideal preparation for life, heaven knows. Maybe something between yours and mine would be best. Some life of great variety—I don't mean the experimental school sort—with some rigour and real encounters. Whatever they might be. More connection with the varieties of reality.' Shrugging, she smiled at Zoe with lively self-derision.

'But still,' Zoe said. 'I know what you mean. Gilded youth always has to learn the hard way.'

With no expression, Anna looked at her. 'So does the other sort.'

The varying degrees of good humour and intelligence Zoe had encountered in her family and friends had appeared to encompass the full range of human nature. Like most people, she naturally believed that what she had not experienced was either non-existent or of no importance. Who ever heard an egoist admit to ignorance? And the Howard circle that she took to be the norm was cosily hedged in, a Garden of Eden in its innocence. Zoe had carelessly thought that everyone belonged there, more or less. A self-contained, undiscovered tribe imagining themselves to be the whole of mankind. How should they not think so, filling as they did a complete floor of the building? Since those days, Zoe had moved to other floors of existence and other tribes. *Now*, she easily recognised those who had never shifted from the place where they started.

They were incapable of believing in the reality of other people and ways, utterly rejected the proposition that there were lives lived out where there was only cruelty, that there were areas inspired by a genius for personal relations, that there were areas of wickedness, of learning and effort, of love, of aggression, of bad temper and malice, where each particular principle ruled and the indigenous subjects praised that one god. There were as many tribes as human types, but the populations varied greatly. It was sad, Zoe thought, to know there were gentle souls marooned amongst the brutal, unable to conceive of a place where gentleness was native to all. The misery of a sour misanthropist among the generous-hearted was also noteworthy.

Stephen had wandered into Howard country, where Zoe too was a foreigner without knowing it. And that was that. She thought: people can be misfits without having anything in common. This isn't always realised. Of course, we did have complementary needs to practise our talents. She had forgotten that.

Anna was saying, 'In offices, places like that, the number of frustrated Machiavellis and Oliviers would stun you. Any larger-than-life figure you can think of has his millions of awful copies. Characters without a stage (except home and work), all having to practise their personalities under the constriction of having to work at something uncongenial in order to eat.'

She stroked Zoe's new grey kitten, rolled a green rubber ball away for it to chase.

'Are women the same?' Zoe wanted to know. In the background, the plumbers' transistor had launched into *Don Giovanni*.

'Oh, women are still in their early days. There isn't very much for them to be like without upsetting preconceptions. Some of them are warriors, too, but mostly they're belly dancers or capable little Victorian mothers. On the other hand,' she said, suddenly penitent, 'I know heroic types of both sexes, who were not only in their imaginations worthy of a better fate, but were really worthy, and really did suffer from great qualities that had no outlet, and it certainly wasn't their fault.

Unless you can call it a fault to be born too soon to be caught up in the general affluence, which younger people think has always been here.'

'Let's not pretend education makes perfect,' Zoe protested, 'if that's what you're thinking of. It's useful or enthralling even, but it doesn't alter the real person. It's interesting. Something your heroic ones ought to have, since they have what counts most in the first place.'

'Not only that I was thinking of. Well-meaning but ignorant families, world wars, moderate poverty, broke their lives.'

Zoe smiled. 'But not their characters?'

'Never their characters, or they wouldn't be my heroic ones.'

'You love the people you love, Anna.'

'I love the people I love. They do tend to be wonderful,' she admitted. 'But I don't change my mind about them. They tend to stay wonderful.'

One of the plumbers arrived, a cheerful ginger young man of twenty-two or -three. 'Could y'give us an idea where the fuse box'd be?' he asked confidingly.

'I'll show you.' Anna jumped up. 'You're supposed to recline, Zo.'

'You like Mozart,' Zoe heard her remark, and the plumber, Mr Horton, replied joyfully. 'You been listening? I got everything on record.'

'You've made a friend.' Over the top of her sunglasses, Zoe peered at her when she returned. 'Another friend. You're like my mother, so sympathetic, and such a good listener.'

'So they tell me. I must take my ears and sympathy away soon.'

'*No*. Lunch is ready in the oven. I thought you might carry it through for us? Anna...' She had no idea how she meant to proceed.

'Yes?' Anna was watching the kitten play with a long thread of wool.

'How's Tom?' Even to herself this sounded abrupt. Zoe felt a slight warmth in her face and ears.

'Tom's all right. Why?'

'I wondered, that's all. What's he doing?'

'Good. Doing good. And most unnatural to him it is, too!' Zoe laughed.

A number of young men and women derisively known to Lily as 'the disciples' had, over a period of years, been spurred to change their ways by observing Russell's ways. Most of them were perplexed to find that a change of occupation was more easily achieved than a change of heart. Like those who choose their clothes with an eye to being taken for someone 'interesting', they were disappointed to find themselves unaltered in the fancy dress of Russell's gestures and concerns. Hills peeped o'er hills, and alps on alps arose. Some turned into friends and associates; others cultivated a rancorous animosity towards him for having unintentionally shown them limitations displeasing to their vanity. Well, *he* was not infallible. *He* was far from perfect. They loathed him.

Tom Hamilton, Anna's Tom, had gone so far as to resign

from a prosperous career in advertising, submit himself to a new training in social work, and to work daily now amongst the aged and hard-pressed.

Anna's fair hair was short with loose curls, beautifully cut in the fashion of the time to make her resemble some romantic Victorian poet. She now pulled at these trained and tended locks in troubled reflection.

'It's the worst possible work for a depressive. He's like Stephen. He hates it. He's sentimental, and there's no room for that sort of feeling in disaster areas.'

Pretending to adjust her sunglasses, Zoe said, 'What do you mean—he's a depressive, like Stephen?'

'Well, only loosely like Stephen. Stephen's brighter, but his moods are more violent.'

'Oh.' Antagonism came surging forth. To cover it, biding for time, Zoe was inspired to listen to her watch. 'Depressive. I never think of anyone close to me in terms like that.' For seconds she prided herself on her self-control, then burst out, 'If anyone could measure what he's had to overcome, it should be you.'

Anna looked into eyes that were angry and defenceless. After a pause, she said, 'He had a hard beginning and never recovered from it. You can admire the way someone meets hard circumstances, but you can't admire him *because* of them.'

'Would compassion be beyond you?'

'I can bully my will, but not my feelings. They're not biddable. If you think yours are, you're kidding yourself.'

'How hard you are.' She sighed. 'You're ghastly. All this

fearful truthfulness.' Her mind wandered these fields of truthfulness spread round her by Anna, and suddenly she was in despair. 'I know. People have to get over things. But what if they don't?'

After another pause, Anna said, 'But about Tom—I hope they'll move him into administration. He'd do very well.'

Not to be diverted, Zoe asked, 'How would you classify me?'

'I wouldn't classify you at all! Don't be offended!'

'No, but what am I?'

Turning her face slightly to one side and smiling, Anna said, 'You're an idealist.'

'And you?'

'A sort of realist.'

'And Lily?'

'An illusionist.'

'And Russell?'

Like someone caught off-guard in a word-association test, Anna halted. 'Oh, Russell...He's someone you need never feel sorry for. And in a sense that's the highest praise you could give.'

Zoe saw what she meant, but in her mind chastised herself for being no closer to the matter urged on her by Stephen— discovering the reason for Anna's alleged sorrow.

'What's Tom, then?' Surely, in spite of the absence of evidence, he must be part of it?

'I've told you—a lost soul. Money's the only thing that rouses the natural man in Tom. Unfortunately, he's been seduced by the company he keeps—by which I mean us—into feeling that there might be *something else in life*. Money chasing seems unworthy, and he's ashamed of it, and it's what he cares about. In advertising, after he met Russell, he worried about his integrity. Now that he's a social worker, he broods about his income.'

'What's wrong with money?' Zoe asked, to be perverse. 'Russell's no pauper. That's why he's free to spend so much time—trying to humanise what's inhuman around the place.'

Anna only looked up into the windy sky. 'Tom isn't Russell.'

'Do you sometimes think it's odd that Russell's stayed outside politics? One of nature's non-joiners. He's probably freer this way. That paper he turns out has quite a list of subscribers! And I don't only mean the numbers.'

'I know.'

'And the things he's done for old people, and the help he's rallied for those poverty-stricken preschool places—none of it's negligible. Yet sometimes I feel he's wasted his life. Do you?...I suppose the people involved wouldn't think so. Does he ever seem lonely to you?'

'Russell?...' Anna let so long a silence accumulate that it was a kind of answer. Still, she stared at the clouds.

Zoe stated, 'Then you'll never marry Tom.'

'Oh, no.'

'You judge him,' Zoe said, like a judge.

'No. I notice. If I see a tiled floor I notice it, but that's not to make a judgment.'

'Wouldn't it be generous to let him go?' In recent years, Zoe had come to identify herself with unrequited and mistaken lovers to such an extent that the idea of what it was permissible to say even to a close friend had temporarily passed her by. She no longer cared very much what she said. Ordinary restraints had less and less meaning for her. Social behaviour was just another way of telling lies.

Without surprise, Anna said, 'He's free. I was gone for a year. He sees other women. I see other men. We've wasted some time together, that's all.'

Giving her a puzzled look, Zoe said, 'Still. When he's with us, I feel sorry for him. If you cared for someone and your feeling wasn't returned, I imagine it would be—anguish—to watch that person with others who mattered more. Crumbs from a banquet to a starving man. Mattered more or with more rights.'

There was a moderately long silence during which Anna pulled on a woollen blazer. 'Getting cold...No one has to bear the sight of me wrapped in the arms of my true love, after all.'

The tone of this statement was rejected by Zoe's mind as beyond analysis. 'No,' she said cautiously, as though she meant the opposite. 'But you're more present when you speak—say, to Russell—than when you talk to Tom.'

'Do you think so?' Anna's tone was abstracted. 'Russell and I never have much to say to each other.' Idly, she lifted one of Zoe's books from the floor and began running a thumbnail across the spine. It made a rasping sound.

Having listened to this phrase a few times, Zoe went on,

'Not Russell in particular. Any of your real friends. Relaxed. Familiar.' Nothing she said was quite right; she felt ill at ease. They both seemed to listen to silent voices.

Then Anna laid the book down again. 'I think you're attributing your own superior feelings to Tom, so that you can feel sorry for him.'

Through narrowed eyes, Zoe considered each of her ten long fingernails. 'When you don't care for someone, it's easy to dismiss his feelings. It's easy to be contemptuous. It's impossible to take seriously any feeling you don't return.'

'Yes. Agreed. 'Twas ever thus. What's to be done about it?' Anna said almost impatiently. Then as if the voices she had heard beneath Zoe's voice suddenly ceased, Anna looked at her with total attention. 'What's made you think of all this? What are you thinking of?'

Glancing away, Zoe said, 'Nothing. A cup of tea. Food. See those clouds! The sky does look exactly like a dome. Was Canada so beautiful with its high mountains and white snow? Your work shot ahead. I thought it could hardly be better, but it is.'

'All this concern for Tom!'

Zoe laughed weakly, guiltily. She felt nothing for Tom, nothing for Stephen, nothing for Anna or anyone. It was only that unrequited love seemed such a waste. Like seeing a whole summer's harvest dumped in the ocean, with so many starving. 'No, but it is sad when things don't work out, isn't it?'

Standing up, Anna looked out over the garden, saw the glitter of water, then went to the door to go inside. 'If you're thinking of food, it's lunch time.' Then she nodded two or three times, 'Yes, it is sad.'

•

'I've known better days,' Russell admitted, at his end of the line.

'What else is wrong?' Zoe wanted to know—meaning, in addition to Lily. In the eight weeks since the girls had gone, Lily had become the chief concern of her family.

'Just a few dramas here at work. I suppose Stephen's told you?…He will.'

Drawing flowers and squares on a scribbler, Zoe sat at home at her desk, listening to Russell's voice.

'He'll have to go to Melbourne in my place because of this. Have lunch with me in town then, and we'll swap news. But look in on Lily this evening, won't you?'

Lily, heavily tranquilised, correctly suspected her husband and everyone close to her of conspiring to wrest from her what they saw as the first stage of a destructive illness. Supplied with drugs by a doctor who had known her all her life, she seldom left her bed.

Now that she was released from the restrictions following her own illness, Zoe jogged along to the other end of the beach daily, ostensibly to discuss work from the office. Her alarm and depression increased with every visit. Too many people had changed. I know no one, she thought. I'm close to no one. No one knows me. Stephen's moods jerked unpredictably from tenderness to abuse, exhausting her capacity to feel surprise.

All she felt was buffeted, battered, cold, apprehensive. Her heart beat heavily day after day. Pity was openly placed on her by those who saw them together. When he tormented her, she had begun to be disagreeable to other people in retaliation. She saw that he was only rarely, rather slyly, aware of his strangeness, as though catching sight of himself out of the corner of his eye, not displeased to find himself so disconcerting yet immune from censure. Could he be held responsible for behaviour stemming from his unconscious? He seemed to delight in the certainty that he could not.

In need of reliability, she had rung Russell one night. Home from a meeting, sitting solitary amongst the furniture, his wife in a drugged sleep upstairs, he told her, 'I've settled down with a whisky bottle. Forgetting it all.' She supposed he meant Lily. He sounded bleak, unrecognisable. As she replaced the receiver Zoe had an image of a black earth in a blackened universe. For some time, pictures like this had been falling on her mind like shadows.

Stephen was lost to her.

Russell's harmless, recuperative evening with the whisky bottle meant nothing, but for the moment, he too had *seemed* lost to her.

Anna had visited David's parents in Canberra for a week, and had then gone on to Melbourne to stay with friends. Now she was in the country at the house of some acquaintance. The odd thing was that she had gone two days after visiting Zoe, without mentioning the possibility beforehand to anyone. The first news of her absence came in a brief note giving details of her holiday itinerary. Since then, not a word.

And Lily, another stranger, a stranger with glazed, unfocussed eyes. The real one, that vibrant, egoistic, entertaining, hectoring, child-fixated, education-worshipping victim of 'psych' lectures, would never have fallen into this disrepair because of plans or persons, however dear, going astray. It was as if a human version of something like a mountain or a cathedral had chosen to destroy itself. Zoe felt the shock renewed every day when she climbed her childhood's stairs to face this alien person. Sleepy, amenable, Lily lay in bed while her mother and Zoe and the housekeeper took turns to sit by her, offering food and drink and attempting light conversation.

Outwardly confident and reassuring, in truth, Zoe shrank from those she knew best. There had been too many changes, and none of them for the better. Her judgment in all things, in all she had known most intimately, on which she had spent her life's best efforts, was wrong. Stephen had tried tenaciously and had at last succeeded in breaking her best beliefs.

And poor Russell! She hated to think how this weird reversal of personality in Lily affected him. Perhaps this was part of growing older, to undergo hideous alterations in the deepest certainties, in love, in lovers, finally in one's self. People should be warned, Zoe thought. Of course, they *were* warned. She had been warned. But some natural law preserved ignorance till the firing squad arrived.

'Where's Stephen?' she asked Russell now, holding the receiver cautiously.

'Lunching with some paper manufacturers. How are you managing without Lily doing her share of the work?'

'We can farm out the actual translating, but the correspondence runs wild unless one of us lives in the office. It should expand or fold up. We've had offers.' Zoe eyed the files on her desk.

'Why not sell it? You've both wanted to for months.'

Zoe gave a sigh. 'Years. I'd really like to. I'll see if I can persuade her to give it some thought. How was she last night?'

'Much the same. Our disastrous daughters. She says she's being punished for having been attached to them beyond reason. She threatens to jump out of the window if I bring a doctor in.'

A silence fell.

'She's half-promised me to come for a swim in the pool tomorrow,' Zoe said.

'I wish she would. When I hear her talking about the way the girls betrayed her...'

Lily was like someone whose entire fortune—money, jewels, landed estates—had been swallowed overnight by a rapacious invader. Too much of herself had been invested in these belongings to allow for any real recovery. It occurred to Zoe that if we lived forever, there would be time to recover from mistakes of twenty years' duration. As it is, we're caught both ways: it's fatal to prune off too large an area of the past, but not bearable to live with large tracts of error, either.

'Yes, there was bad organisation somewhere,' Russell commented, and they both laughed because there was nothing else to do. 'Have you heard from Anna?'

'Only that note.' Zoe hesitated to say more, searching for the generosity to spare him her troubled thoughts. 'I'd better let you go...'

But Russell went on, 'Stephen said Alan Falkland called round last night to show you those dummy jackets.'

'Yes. They weren't much good. Just as well you didn't commission him.'

'The lack of appreciation isn't mutual. You're always being dragged into the conversation when he comes here.'

Zoe gave a groan. When Stephen had said something to this effect the previous evening after Alan left, their eyes had endured a brief meeting. While she cleaned make-up from her face, Stephen stood behind her, watching her mirrored reflection.

'At least you used not to be so self-important.'

She felt frightened. 'What do you mean?'

'You usedn't to be so self-important. That tone of voice, the voice of the expert, when Alan was asking you about the so-called film festival. You can swallow any amount of flattery, I'll say that for you. You're not too fussy about the source. You wallow in it, don't you?'

'My tone of voice?' Zoe tried to remember. Somewhere in her chest a tiny trickle of fear ran. Long ago, she had learned to discount these verbal assaults, but his motive in uttering them touched her mind like a nightmare. Was he right? She felt herself so demoralised that she had no way of knowing.

'You jumped at the chance when he wanted to interview you about the famous Joseph coming out for the festival, didn't you? It's lovely to see your name in the paper.'

Her hands moved stiffly and slowly over her face. His rightness or wrongness were not in question: he had laid a charge against her, and had found a legitimate reason for his detestation. She felt he had no such justification. They were agreed in detesting the person she had become. She had laid too great a burden on someone not strong enough to bear it. She had expected too much of his nature. Also, it was so much harder for him to hurt her now: when he needed so much to disparage and destroy, it seemed cruel to grudge him whatever reason he could find.

She said lightly, 'No one will blame you for my self-importance. Be sure of that.'

'Pontificating as if the fate of nations hung on your judicious words, or your presence at some parochial film festival.'

She had said Joseph was original. Pretty inflammable stuff! Still talking, Stephen walked up and down behind her where she sat at the dressing table; and she listened with a sort of scientific accuracy, trying to breathe so as not to disturb the cold, hard, angular thing that had been inserted behind her ribs.

'All of you Howards fancy yourselves as public figures. Your mother and father did. Russell's always on some platform crusading. And you last night, talking to Falkland. These ponderous pauses. These weighty deliveries. I hope you don't think he was interested in what you were saying? We know where his interests lie, don't we?'

Zoe said nothing. Chill, narrow knives had been skilfully slid into her mind. There was no thought without pain.

'It was one of the things I noticed about you when you came back from Paris—that a little local publicity left you untouched. I admired that. Because you do know, don't you, that you only have to be a horse or a footballer to rate space in the press. You only need a rich daddy. You should watch it,' he said sharply. 'You've changed.'

Zoe laughed.

'If I've noticed, you can be sure other people have.' Then he felt he had said enough and, still breathing rather heavily with excitement, began to get ready for bed.

On her way to the shower, Zoe paused and looked back. 'You're not conceivably jealous, so what is it really?'

'You'd like to know, wouldn't you?' He took off his shoes.

The confusion of his mind confused her. She said nothing. In the shower her hands were useless and frail, the fingers pale, their grip feeble. The cake of soap slipped from them again and again. They grew daily paler and weaker like the hands of a sick person.

What next? He might prolong the joust. He might remonstrate with her gently and wisely about her character. Always surprising, he might act as if they were the truest of true lovers. She had given him such confidence in his power over her, a flattering confidence in the resilience of her feeling for him.

Now, on the telephone, she said to Russell, 'I hope Alan doesn't come round again. He and Stephen bring out the worst in each other. Refereeing isn't my idea of a good time. And if he comes when I'm alone, he criticises Stephen.'

How she had come to give time to Alan Falkland, she could scarcely recall. He was about thirty-five, married; he had rough curly brown hair and sleepy eyes. He was relaxed. She saw that they could like each other, so she fended him off. (Besides, ultimately, everyone was like Stephen, however they covered it up. *He* thought so, and she believed him.) But when, risking a few steps on quicksand, Alan uttered slanted words against Stephen, her passivity surprised them both. She had not the energy to dispute his words. Once, she might have been awarded a Nobel Prize for loyalty. Now, this immutable quality had melted like ice in the sun. She had lost heart. Hard words, silent hatred, had caused it to vanish, taking a large part of her intelligence. This was why she could behave so strangely and dangerously, why she was acquiescent when Alan Falkland disparaged her husband.

Russell said now, 'I think you're hard on Alan. I like him.'

Disingenuously, she answered, 'You can have him.' It was unlike Russell to ring to gossip away the time.

'Tom Hamilton raced in this morning. He'd just been to the family solicitor, and his uncle's estate's cleared up at last. Tom comes into a whacking great sum, and on the strength of it, he's writing to ask Anna to marry him.'

'He *told* you?'

'Yes.'

'He never gives up. I don't think much of his chances. What did you say?'

'I wished him luck.'

'Oh, *did* you?' she asked, in surprise.

Then Russell was called downstairs to adjudicate in the packing department, and they said goodbye. And Zoe sat where she was, not moving, encircled by a moving film of fallen forests, of the ruins of blackened smoking cities. She saw a figure drowning, one arm outstretched. She saw a closed door. There was no going back through the door and, most horribly, no desire to go back. And there again was the blackened, reeking, devastated plain that was once a city. Like an addict who languished for the drug that ate her up, she could not have too much of these sights. They were the most real things of all. When, arduously, she was obliged to tear herself from them, she decided vaguely that they must be symbols. She had never been good at symbols. Other people saw them everywhere. Now of their own accord these compelling visions had come to teach her something. And exhausting as they were in a way, they were also a last goodbye from innocence and other beautiful and eternal states.

At her desk in her work room in her comfortable house on the harbour of the world's twenty-eighth largest city, with a population more or less equal to that of Rome, Zoe sat amongst the wreckage and held tightly to the images her mind produced in its efforts to help her survive.

She had the impression that they would soon disappear, these otherworldly images, and then she would be left in a foreign country. Forty. Physically, she felt no different from the way she'd felt at twenty; her general aspect was far from ravaged. But an idea, or an illusion, or her very self, had been lost or killed. And she could not shake off the conviction that what was gone was the very best she had been able to offer to the world.

Consciously, she brushed some hair from her cheek, and stared at the mute painting above the desk. Dogs barked in the distance. The encircling screens receded. Going to the open windows, she saw the kitten washing himself fastidiously on the bright green grass. Sometimes it seemed that nothing much had happened. There was only a vague distress, the dreamlike sensation of having mislaid something vital. Some messenger from life stood before her with a telegram reading: *you have lost your life* or *sadness unto death*. It seemed dramatic, and half-touched her, this eternal telegram. Yet really, apart from the sensation of irretrievable loss, there was nothing wrong at all.

•

Tom Hamilton arrived just after lunch to tell Zoe his news—the large legacy finally free of entanglements, and Tom a relatively rich man, about to ask Anna to marry him. This piece of luck, in the area of greatest importance to him, had given Tom colossal confidence. It was clear that he felt himself and his new money to be quite irresistible. He had assumed that what was of prime importance to him necessarily mattered most to everyone else. And Zoe saw that this was what baffled us so in our dealings with each other, so rarely knowing what the springs of life were for another person.

'Come and sit down, Tom. What would you like? A drink? Coffee?'

'Nothing thanks, Zo. I'm on my way to Manly. But you're on my side, aren't you? You've all wanted to see Anna settled for a long time.'

'Heavens, Tom...I wish you well.' She swallowed. 'I wish you both well. But as for seeing Anna settled—I don't know that any of us ever thought of it like that.'

'Oh!' Tom looked dashed and felt nervously for his cigarettes. 'I thought you'd be pleased.'

'Well, I am pleased about your legacy, but as for Anna— my pleasure's not strictly relevant.' This was distinctly awkward. Why had Anna allowed him to feel this amount of assurance? Why had he naïvely confided in everyone before even writing to her?

'You've always been encouraging,' he accused her.

'I like you,' she cried. 'I'm not *dis*couraging now. I'm just older. A few years ago I knew what was best for everyone, now I don't. Everything's more mysterious, not less so. That's all.' As for the encouragement that misled people, this was a family failing she and Russell shared.

'Oh, I see.' Tom thawed and grinned with relief, a lean, brown man in early middle age, black patent hair, very expensive, well-chosen clothes. Zoe wondered almost enviously if Anna placed enough value on his good nature, if she knew how it ought to be valued.

'You're worried in case she refuses.'

Zoe said evasively, 'Whatever happens will be best in the long run. She'll be back for Lily's birthday dinner.'

'What sort of philosophy is that?' Tom rounded his eyes, and she smiled. 'A good question!'

•

At dawn the cicadas started up like an alarm clock and woke the birds seconds later. They began raggedly like young amateurs, practising, and then they were in full voice. Stephen and Zoe lay listening.

They went along the beach and swam in Russell's pool before anyone was awake. The sun rose swiftly and built a shifting honeycomb of light on the green floor of the pool. The early morning had a glassy fragility, and Zoe felt the link between herself and Stephen to have that same extreme fragility and transparency; a breath could shatter it. Stephen churned through the water. She shivered and pulled on her towelling coat, prudently absent from past and future.

At breakfast, Stephen ran a forefinger down the back of her left hand, unwilling as she was to disturb by so much as a word the tender concord in which they rested now, forgiven and forgiving. Of course, this mood was vulnerable, too, if memories were not held rigid. To remember that this luminous mutual silent companionship had come and gone countless times was to prepare for its absence.

Stephen switched the wireless on. They half-listened to

the news. Like everyone else, they heard too much bad news about the world every day. This was the usual thing: wars, the number killed in recent actions, a bank robbery, a ship sinking in the Atlantic, a cyclone in the north, disarmament talks breaking down, cancer research, death of a well-known public servant.

'Tim Coleman. A heart attack!'

'You'll have to tell your father,' Stephen said. The dead man had been Mr Howard's friend.

Twenty years earlier, Coleman was the defendant in a sensational political case, and found not guilty. But there were terrible betrayals.

'I met him in the street last month,' she said. 'He looked very white. We went straight into the middle of the case, as if it was still going on.'

'He thought of nothing else.'

'And everyone was indulgent and patronising.' For years she had heard the talk: 'Poor old Coleman. He's very bitter. Of course, he was badly treated.'

He seemed to be plotting to alter the past, like a ghost. There was a real injustice done him, and the whole city argued and speculated. He was the man of the moment. But afterwards no one wanted to stand with him on the hillside looking back. Every morsel had been chewed from that old story. Passers-by were relieved to patronise him because their own disasters were of the less public sort, cherished secrets, like hit-and-run accidents no one knew about.

'Was he married?' Stephen asked.

'No. And the people he *did* count on weren't to be counted on.'

Ah-ah. Unwise. Too close for comfort. They gave each other a cagey, warning look and busied themselves buttering toast.

'Let's not listen to any more of that.' Zoe nodded at the wireless and Stephen silenced it gladly. The world weighed on him.

As Russell was caught up by the crisis at work, Stephen was leaving for Melbourne this morning in his place. There had been a road accident. One of the boys at the press had been charged with negligent driving. Stephen had implied that the whole business was Russell's fault, but Zoe had asked no questions and turned her eyes away from the curious glee in his.

After breakfast, she drove him out to the airport. 'I'll keep my fingers crossed till you land,' she said, as she used to say.

'In the hope that I'll crash?' He glanced up from his wallet with a smile.

Zoe looked at his cheeks, his thin nose, at the line between his brows, the odd smile in his eyes. He looked prosperous, and very clean, and relentless, and he smelled very faintly of cleanliness and after-shave lotion.

He went on, 'I may have to come back from Canberra by train. By the time I get up there the pilots will be on strike.'

'Yes, I saw that.'

'You're not nervous staying alone in the house, are you? Because plenty of people would come and keep you company, if you are.'

Zoe smiled at this, with irony and affection. True, there had been robberies in the area. But what could anyone walking in out of the night do to harm her? No stranger had ever harmed her. It was incredible to realise how far she now was out of harm's way.

'I've said something funny.'

'Pretty. When you come back, I think we should talk to each other.' Because it was unpremeditated, such an alarming and final statement, Zoe could scarcely see. The road ahead, the buildings, Stephen at her side, were visible in flashes as though lights were being turned on and off.

'What about?'

But they were arriving at Mascot. Zoe looked for a parking meter and found a vacant one. She said nothing more, but when the car was parked and they sat silent, Stephen said, 'If you must.'

●

Next morning she woke alone in the big bed. The telephone was ringing.

Lily's new laboured voice spoke to her. 'Russell wanted me to ring you early before you started to walk over. He said you're still partly convalescent, so I should make the effort to visit you for a change.'

'Rush over. That's lovely,' she said, instantly abandoning sleep.

No Mrs Trent coming to clean today. No Stephen coming

home. Zoe made coffee and took it to her desk to do some work before Lily arrived, only pausing on the way to examine the view. Before she had finished half a page, Lily arrived.

'I didn't hear you for the typewriter.' Zoe jumped up to welcome her. This was the first time Lily had left the house since the girls' departure, an event. She allowed herself to be led by the hand to the sofa.

Sitting half-turned away from her desk, Zoe watched her with hidden wariness. But Lily had altered again since her telephone call this morning. She accepted a cup of coffee, and rustled the morning newspaper lying next to her, inclined to discuss current affairs. Zoe was amazed. Nothing but tragedy and broken-hearted mothers for weeks, now Lily was saying, 'Did you read that piece about knowledge being injected into rats?'

'Alarming.'

'You mean, if you work for twenty years to learn something, you resent another person—'

'—or rat—'

'—learning the same thing overnight.'

'Who's going to be God? Who's going to choose what's injected? What happens to original thought?'

'You're against progress.'

'I'm against human automata. What happens if you bypass human nature? Where are you going in such a hurry with your instant knowledge?'

'You're so intense and emotional and personal,' Lily said.

Zoe paused to reject several replies. It was years since she had felt free to trample on people's feelings, to lash out with spirited attacks.

'Because I think it matters,' she said. 'Lily. You're at a concert. A violinist. The sound is flawless. You know he's been given a pill or a needle and handed a violin for the first time in his life. He has no feeling for the music. He's a freak. How do you feel about the performance?'

Lily reflected. 'What's he playing?'

Zoe laughed. 'I'm wasting my time.'

Suddenly casting off her recognisable self, Lily said— black misery in the tone, blood-curdling self-pity in the eyes: 'We had a letter from the girls yesterday. Set for life. Happy as larks.'

'Try to be glad about it for your own sake, if not for theirs.' She wanted to evaporate. The idea of being pulverised yet again by Lily's obsession made her feel persecuted.

Giving her a glance of purest hatred, Lily turned ostentatiously to stare at the well-known view, which filled the room like a rather too-literal painting of itself.

Left to her own devices, Zoe contemplated the work spread out on her desk.

'If they had an ounce of family feeling they'd never have gone away.' Despite her obvious desire to snub her unsympathetic sister-in-law, Lily had to speak. 'I could have followed my own career, and had a vastly different life. They don't think of that. With their scholarships and what they inherited from my father they can do anything they want.' Her sandalled feet, her bare tanned legs, were disposed at awkward angles.

Aware that reasonable and consolatory speeches would be avidly collected as further proof of the world's cruelty and heartlessness, Zoe said, with a greater show of energy and goodwill than she felt, 'But all's not lost. You've got Russell. Your mother and the aunts are still next door. You can still take up your work.'

'Russell! What does it matter to him? He's always been more interested in mankind. Strangers and causes have always meant more to him. The press works because he's got the best staff in Sydney, and he keeps them because of the co-operative thing. Stephen slaves, but it's almost a hobby for Russell. He's always at meetings. Oh, he's worked hard. God knows that's true! And he's influenced a lot of people to do fine things. But he's no time or interest to spare for his family.'

Zoe sighed audibly. 'Oh, Lily. You can't expect me to agree with you. You don't even mean it. If you'd wanted to, you could have been part of everything he's done.'

But Lily's face was set in rigid lines. 'I mean it, though it doesn't matter much—about Russell. The children are every-thing. I've always put them first. Some women are like that. You wouldn't understand.'

Zoe felt she understood too well. Lily had tried her for years to live through the girls, lived on their high spirits, emotions, the events of their lives. She had seen them fade under the intensity of their mother's attention. The difference between being idolised and plagued can be very small.

Moving to a comfortable chair opposite Lily, Zoe said, 'What I do understand is that at any point in a woman's life she may come across something like a cement pyramid in the middle of the road. Another person. People. She's capable of sitting there, convinced that it would be impossible to forsake her position, till it becomes a private Thermopylae. This sort of block was probably designed for the survival of our species, but the cost's high. What makes men superior is that they don't—*on the whole*—stop functioning forever because of another person. They lack this built-in handicap, and are they lucky!' Half-laughing, she added, 'I can't bear sweeping statements. Contradict me!'

With dulled censorious eyes, Lily waited for her to stop, then a startling malevolence brightened her face. 'They're beginning to wonder about the shortage of letters. I've written once since they left.'

Russell had told Zoe this, and Vanessa had written to her, too, asking for unbiased news of her mother.

'That's vindictive, Lily. Why spoil their first months and make yourself unhappy?'

'Oh yes, I'm vindictive. I please myself for once. That's vindictive.'

Zoe went to the open door to gather some strength from the air and trees. Out on the bay, three speedboats were pursuing some purposeful course. The third seemed to be operating for the benefit of a camera crew, massively equipped, filming the other two.

Over her shoulder she said to Lily, 'This looks like the birth of a television commercial.'

Lily came to watch the invasion of their peaceful bay with

a sort of critical resignation. A gold-patterned butterfly wavered past close by.

'Have you had any breakfast?...Neither have I. Come and let's eat something.'

'When in doubt, produce food. I used to do that. What they could put away for dinner!'

Catching her rueful, reminiscent expression now that she had forgotten for the moment to extort commiseration Zoe did pity her at last, and thought it regrettable that everybody's happiness seemed to flourish best on someone else's murdered heart. Though, as she started to prepare and cook mushrooms and eggs, she told herself that that was an extreme, florid and probably untrue way of stating the case. Still, there did appear to be a sort of waste not, want not policy which everybody made use of. Like coral, she decided, stirring, leaning against the stove. They talked about nature's prodigality and lavish wastefulness, but—depending which eye you chose to close— it could seem there was thrift and husbandry everywhere.

Lily poured the orange juice. 'I'm only interrupting your day's work, coming over like this. Russell felt I shouldn't stay home brooding. Easier to come than argue. Not that he would argue. Not that anyone would. Everyone makes allowances.' This came out viciously, and Zoe flinched, and frowned at the mushrooms as she served them.

'It's not badly meant. You've had some sort of psychic shock. It's hard to get over it.'

As though a nerve had been touched, Lily's face moved. 'How do you know that? Without children.'

'You mothers *are* egotistical. There are other blows in life.' Zoe pulled out a stool and sat opposite Lily at the counter.

'You haven't told me yet to pull myself together.' Lily started to eat.

'I daresay you will, just the same.'

'But you don't think it's justified—the way I am?'

'I think it's a pity. You're the one who knows if it's justified. And I don't suppose even you know how far you're prepared to take it. It isn't a matter of conscious decisions. I mean—the decision to recover comes from a place not open to influence.'

Leaning to one side, Zoe slid two blue-and-white Swedish cups across the counter and switched off the percolator. 'You just have to wait it out. It probably is important to make a few efforts in case they do get through to headquarters.' Her manner was tentative, but she did believe that everything everybody did mattered.

Lily greeted this with a satisfied, spiteful smile. 'I've been delivering unwanted advice for years. If it lands back on my doorstep when I'm least able to put up with it, that's only fair. You think I'm unreasonable.'

Stephen had taught Zoe patience. She said, 'The way you feel and anyone who wants you to be reasonable exist on different planets.'

Eating what was on her plate, Lily listened with unnatural intentness. 'I'm like a politician waiting for the result of a referendum. Very sensitive to public opinion. And, I must say, you seem to understand. Why today?'

Alarmed to find herself under scrutiny, Zoe shifted on her stool. 'I don't know. It's easy to talk to you. You're more like yourself.'

'Ah,' Lily said, with comprehension. 'Russell tells you I'm usually all doped up? Well, I did take stuff for a week or two, then I stopped. He didn't bother to notice the difference. None of you did.'

'Oh.' Eyes down, Zoe crunched rather sullenly through a piece of toast and pushed her plate away. It was worse than she had imagined, if Lily had lost touch to this extent; if she could lie about something so obvious. Though Zoe had come a long way since the days when she believed the truth was always best; though she was persuaded now that sometimes, unhappily, it had to take second place to another person's vital illusions; though cleverer people could make an addiction to it seem all that was boring; nevertheless, she had a passion for it, and if the roof fell and the city fell, she could not suppress it. So she munched gloomily and looked down.

Lily put some sugar in her coffee. 'He thinks I'm lying about it.'

Again, Zoe felt herself sinking almost physically. 'How could he, if it weren't so?' she asked faintly. 'How could he make a mistake like that?'

'How could I? Assuming I'm in my right mind.'

Zoe moved a hand expressively. 'That's different. You're under stress. He would never disbelieve you without reason.'

'You idealise everyone, Zo.'

She met Lily's eyes. Anna had said that, too.

'We tell each other small lies from time to time,' Lily said. 'He just happens to be wrong now. You look surprised. Nothing enormous. Conspiracies with the girls.'

Sitting there, with her heels hooked over the brass-bound spar of the stool, Zoe believed her, but felt disenchanted. She believed everyone she liked. She never expected lies. They always bowled her over, and she never expected them next time, in spite of her conviction that Stephen was right to suspect and denigrate everything human when the mood took him, in spite of her willingness sometimes to agree with him.

'If they're such small lies, are they worth the trouble?' she asked now, thoroughly put out.

'You idealise everyone,' Lily repeated censoriously.

'You've seemed—unfamiliar. I suppose that's what made Russell think—all of us...'

'He couldn't believe it was "only the girls". Only the girls!'

'No.' Zoe began to feel worn down. 'But when weeks went by without any sign that you were—accepting the way things were, and so *different*, we thought you must be still taking stuff.'

'Everyone believed Russell, that's all.'

'We've all got eyes. The thought that you were drugged to insensibility was no more impossible than that you were...I can see now the effect the girls have had, and I'm sorry. But it isn't the end of the world.' Zoe had no idea how wise it was to talk like this to Lily, but you could tiptoe round for just so long.

Resting her elbows on the counter, Lily clasped her hands and leaned her chin on the tangle of fingers. She half-laughed. 'In my palmier days, I was always making people count their blessings, reminding them about starving Indians, and girls dying of abortions, and people being burned alive in wars. High-minded when nothing was wrong with my life.'

It was a fact that as a lecturer she had analysed her students, and as a mother her daughters, right out of her life. And self-righteously she used the tragedies of others as if she had invented them herself as moral tales.

Zoe said, 'My unscientific mind thinks, "What would I want if I were Lily, apart from what's not possible?"'

'And what does it answer?'

'It might say, "I'd want someone to *realise*..." I'd want the girls—and since that's impossible, I'd want Russell to realise. I'd want to be understood, I suppose.'

Lily said flatly, 'That's what I must learn to do without.'

In the following silence, Zoe scraped plates and ran hot water and thought of Russell. He seemed to have adjusted easily to Lily's altered state. Was he as unaccountable as every-one else? Was he like Lily—with theory and practice running parallel but never meeting? Even yesterday it would have been inconceivable that she should doubt him. But now...Unexpect-edly, it had started to rain. Zoe liked rain. It reminded her of Europe, the razor's edge, life lived to the hilt.

'But that's wrong,' she said suddenly. 'What I was just saying. What would being understood do for you, if *still* you didn't have your way? It only matters that *you* should work out how to accept changes you don't like.'

Drying and stacking plates, Lily looked mulish. 'Easy to say. Why should I?'

Zoe refrained from swearing. 'Because you must. You haven't been singled out. I must. Russell must. Everyone has to, sooner or later. We all misjudge things, all make mistakes. And if you aren't understood, you're not unique in that!' The awareness that she was trying to argue Lily into an attitude she had failed to achieve herself was not helpful. 'You could only have had your way at the expense of Vanessa and Caroline, and that wouldn't have pleased you. So don't try to spread the punishment round by destroying yourself. Because that's what you're doing.'

In a chastened voice, Lily said, 'It was so unexpected.'

For a minute or so, they both attended fiercely to unimportant tasks with taps, crumbs and tea towels, then they went inside to Zoe's work room and she flung her arms up as though to cast off physically so much preoccupation and unhappiness. 'Anyway, it isn't the end of you. Nothing's been taken away from you. You've probably been added unto.' She spoke with a sort of mesmerising conviction to cover what might be a large piece of misinformation. 'Experience! That's what you're here for.'

Laughing, Lily sank back into the sofa. 'Thanks for the news! I've often wondered.' Her expression had undergone a subtle change. She began to look relaxed, as though the obsession that was her illness had started to retreat. Catching the sound of its withdrawal, she declared, 'I might survive yet.'

'Please do! Because look at all this work!' Zoe gave the desk and its deep papers an anxious glance. 'Oh, *let's* sell the Bureau, Lily.' They exchanged a hopeful look, and within three minutes had worked out the campaign for its disposal, and Lily agreed that she would go back to university to teach, learn, or sweep, if necessary.

'We can announce all this at your birthday dinner,' Zoe said when they parted. 'With everyone assembled—Stephen back from Melbourne, and Anna home, too.'

•

On the bus, a dark-haired girl opposite Zoe nursed a plump and beautiful baby boy. Now and then she would snatch his right hand in hers and give it a smacking kiss. Sometimes she kissed the top of his head—another explosive sound. Magnanimously, the baby sat on her lap permitting these tributes while he watched everything in front of him with the intelligent detachment of a well-fed king.

Leaving this Arcadian scene reluctantly, Zoe pushed her way up the crowded street to the restaurant where she was meeting Russell for lunch. The placards of competing newspapers tried to startle and shock with headlines that changed from one street corner to the next. WAR EXPANDS. MINING SHARES——WHOOPEE! WALL STREET DEPRESSED. DRUGS——PARENTS IN TEARS.

Buildings Zoe had known all her life had disappeared since the previous week. The wreckers were out; cranes hung over the city. Scaffolding that had come to seem a permanent hazard to pedestrians had been whisked away to reveal skyscrapers, fountains, minatory sculpture. Naming the restaurant where he had booked a table, Russell had added the qualification, 'If it's still there.'

Now they had eaten in this comfortable and quiet basement, and Zoe had heard of the events of the printery, to describe which, Russell had ostensibly arranged today's appointment. She was glad to see him, but thought the reason for their meeting unconvincing.

There had been a near-tragedy. Two weeks earlier, at the request of a welfare officer, he had employed a boy named Frank as a packer. Russell had promised to inspire the boy to stay on the rocky narrow path by providing vaudeville and dancing girls, and already he gave signs of settling down to collect a gold watch on his retirement. In the course of giving some attention to Frank, Russell had inadvertently withdrawn some from a similar castaway known as Bob, famous for his talent for wrecking public telephones. Bob had been at the press for three months, had had his hair cut, started a technical college course, and appeared to have seen a great light in regard to his future.

Disagreeably surprised by Russell's interest in the newly arrived Frank, he waited for ten days in vain for his restoration to centre stage, then wrecked the most expensive machine he could approach, swallowed or injected some enlivening poison, climbed into his car and knocked down a child on a pedestrian crossing. The girl's arm was broken, and Bob was charged. Traffic and even drug offences took decades to reach the courts, Russell said. Meantime, Bob had said enough in his vocabulary of a hundred words to show whose the fault really was. Translated, his complaint against Russell said: hesitate to do this to someone else. The withdrawal is worse than never having had the attention. All but the lamest dogs feel singled out for their unique qualities. The turning away is recognised as: *what could such as you give me?*

'Russell!' Zoe gazed at him in wonderment. Piqued and out to make him sorry, like anyone thwarted, the boy had certainly been. 'But you're elevating irresponsibility and peevishness and wounded vanity into high drama! All this remorse! What's wrong? Something else must be wrong. What is it?' She spoke rapidly, then regretted it. Russell said nothing, filled her glass with wine.

To plaster over the conspicuous crack of his silence, she reminded him that the press had always had its delinquents. Incidents like this were commonplace. If you made efforts on behalf of other people, you also took risks, but that was generous.

Denying this with a shake of his head, Russell drank some wine and watched his sister.

Zoe found his crime difficult to believe in. 'You puzzle me. I can't understand you. This must be one of the least sensational events of your whole life.' No one succeeds everywhere. It was one of Russell's strengths that defeat did not defeat him. He seemed sustained in a way that other people were not. Yet this fact—what they could observe in him—sustained others. An eager and undefended responsiveness to individuals, new moments, gave his attention its high value. It was positively alluring, Zoe thought, to anyone on the side of life. Staring deep in his eyes, Zoe was suddenly made so happy by the very fact of his existence, that she felt a wholly unreasonable surge of optimism.

'You look very sunny for someone so puzzled.' Russell smiled at her smile. 'Have a peppermint.' He said, 'About Lily,' and Zoe thought: *this* is why we met, not the other.

'That was another large error of judgment, giving you the idea that she was an addict. My attention was somewhere else. *Not* with the boys at the press, either. You're right about that.'

None of this was easy to refute. Zoe said resolutely, touching an earring, 'Anyway, she'll be happy when she gets back to work.'

'What about you, Zo? Any way of returning to—the cinema?' He was gently comic, not to pin her down.

'Oh, I should think so,' she said airily, inspecting her empty cup and his and pouring more coffee. Her future was in the past. However, it seemed best to disguise this from Russell.

'Are you still interested?'

'Oh,' she said again.

Abruptly, he asked, 'Have you heard from Stephen?'

'Every evening. Hasn't he spoken to the office? Do you want me to give him a message?'

'No, we've talked several times. He says everyone in Melbourne is busy playing the stock market and making money on real estate. Lily's said something about going abroad. I suppose Stephen wouldn't like it if you went, too? What does he think about the Bureau sale?'

In the dim light of the restaurant, seated as they were at

right angles to each other, it had been easy to avoid meeting eyes. Now Zoe turned to face him. 'He doesn't mind.' She looked into Russell's eyes with dread: the status quo was unbearable, and the thought of change was unbearable. Her store of hope had been used up; Old Mother Hubbard's cupboard was bare. It was beyond her powers to imagine a good change.

'*I* wouldn't like it if I went abroad, too. I wouldn't want to go without him. Perhaps our only trouble'—she smiled and deepened her voice—'if you could call it trouble, is my defective time sense. I'm sure the cat and I feel the same way about time. If Stephen's relaxed and happy and we're enjoying life, it's forever as far as I'm concerned. Then, if he's disagreeable, that's forever, too. I can't see past it. So I fall into that well-known Slough of Despond.'

Elbow on table, she tapped her forehead lightly with the inside of her wrist. 'What's wrong with the way my mind functions? I can *see* this, but I can't do anything about it.'

Russell looked at her lowered head. 'I think we'd have to diagnose it as love.'

'Ah, doctor!' Half-laughing, then sighing, Zoe brushed a hand over her skirt. 'Is that what it is? After all this time. It feels more like dementia. No, we're all right. It's only—I've expected some state of permanent perfection in life, which isn't reasonable. But why are the expectations built in?' She glanced up into Russell's blue eyes.

'At a guess—and if you don't like it, I'll refer you to a specialist—I'd say, so that you would do some striving.'

Zoe fell back against the seat. 'Strive! Let that be my epitaph: She strove. You could also put on my tombstone: Pride goes before a fall. Look before you leap. And, above all, Don't put all your eggs in one basket. The wisdom of the prophets. We should study them more.'

'Doctor of Proverbs. The idea opens up, as they say, a whole new world. They're all true. The contradictions don't matter.'

'It's only—when you hear anyone rave on about the problems of youth, you want to say: wait till they're adults! As if "growing up" finished when you were twenty-one. Or forty. It shakes you to find you could have been so wrong about the most important thing in your life. It must happen to a lot of people. They probably don't make such a fuss.'

'If they don't make a commotion about the most important thing, they might as well be dead,' Russell said. 'Not that I see any sign of one now. Stephen…We've worked together all these years. He doesn't always approve of me, but we've got on well. I know he has these black moods. I've sometimes wondered if the press isn't a restricted sort of field for him. A good half of my time goes on other work. If he feels he's been left to carry the baby, he's right. We've even tried to even it up financially. He's never complained. In all the other work, he's been indispensable. We've had a lot of fun.'

Silent, large-eyed, Zoe listened wistfully. After a second's time lag, she quickly returned his smile.

Russell said, 'But there you are. He's my closest friend, and your husband, and we both know he's difficult. You knew that before you married him.'

Like flame along a fuse wire, indignation ran through Zoe's mind and heart. Could he dare to criticise Stephen? Moving slightly away from him, she asked somehow punctiliously, 'What does that mean?'

For a moment Russell regarded her—not the shadowed eyes, the painted face, the lovely, expensive-looking woman there for all to see, but the person she was and would be whatever her circumstances or age. 'Difficult means difficult. How old was he when you married? Thirty-one? Thirty-two? What went before did too much damage ever to be reversed completely—his parents, that poor destructive woman the house revolved around. He experienced evil at an age when you probably couldn't spell it. Then the sweating away at night for years to get his degree, and the isolation. It wouldn't have affected everyone the same way, but it harmed him. It's a cliché, and it's a fact.'

'Anna said something like that once—about evil. But she's not difficult, and she had longer there.'

'No.' Russell hesitated. He closed his eyes and rubbed them with his fingers. 'No. But that's not the point.'

'What is the point, then?'

'That you're always going to have to make allowances. By which I only mean—to remember all this.'

She frowned. 'You're preaching. I do remember. Most of the time.' Then she sighed with a sort of despairing irritability, and looked at the white tablecloth, the silver sugar bowl. Her mind surged. Unreasonably, she said, 'Wouldn't it have been helpful if you'd told me this before we were married?'

'Ask yourself.'

Reluctantly she granted his point. 'But I might have acted differently at some stage,' she added with an uprush of resentment.

Russell said nothing.

She said naïvely, 'I thought I knew what he was like. I thought I could make him happy, and that he would be like himself.'

Now she realised that she had shared the common illusion that if someone were only 'himself', instead of an imitation of what he could be, he would be fulfilled, more likeable, cleverer, happier, good, better, best. That the mask might sometimes be superior to what lay beneath was an idea that had only recently occurred to her.

'He thought so, too, for a long time. He *was* happy, but something went wrong. Probably my fault.' Clearly, she had been excessive in so many ways—giving too much attention, noticing too much, caring too much. 'I overdo things,' she confessed glumly.

She had waited for him to declare the emergency ended, to announce the beginning of a new regime, to promise that some weight of whose crushing nature she gradually became aware, would be equally shared. Perhaps he was never conscious that she had made any special efforts on his behalf. There was something unnamed, but felt, that she had never expected to have to give up forever. Permanent nurse, analyst, leader and guide, she had never intended to be. Mistaking neurosis for strength, suppressing anything in herself that might damage his self-esteem, she had expected an equal partnership.

'I've been unwise. So be it.'

'I did warn you that you were taking on someone a little more complex than the boy next door. It was presumptuous, and you told me so in a loud voice. But I wondered if two quite different people mightn't have made you both happier.'

'Strangely enough,' she said, in a hard voice, 'that thought has crossed my mind, too. We'll never know,' she said flatly. 'What sort of person—for Stephen?'

Russell glanced at her sideways, and then looked straight ahead into the spacious gloom of the low-ceilinged restaurant. 'Your opposite. Someone more like himself. Someone unluckier, less intense, less passionate, with less enthusiasm. Or someone impervious. I don't know.'

As he spoke, Zoe slid the side of her forefinger across her parted teeth, nervously. She felt pale, as if her blood had gone away. 'Well. It doesn't sound gay. But I know what you mean. My happy youth's always been like a colour bar between us. I was the negro. As you say, if we were more alike, it mightn't have mattered so much. But if you instinctively see from such different angles, and you've had such different experiences, it certainly makes a gulf. He thought me juvenile, and I thought his sense of the ridiculous must have atrophied in childhood.'

'You say he *thought*...'

Zoe gave a half-smile. 'I've graduated. We made our own misfortunes and had those to share. A bond. Like the Konrad

Lorenz triumph ceremony. But the funny thing is he doesn't like the sad version now that he's got it.'

'You're his life.'

She looked at him. 'Am I? He's mine. But is that a good thing? He's sometimes so shut away, or so deliberately cruel, that I can't always believe it, much as I want to. I'm sometimes terrified.' It frightened her even to say it.

Russell said, 'Not everyone can bear to be loved, Zo.'

And Zoe, who had thought so much, had never thought of this. It struck her as blasphemy and a denial of faith might have struck an innocent and devout religious.

'This isn't news.'

'No.' But she was stupefied, sat really as though he had clubbed her about the head.

It was true, what he said. Being able to love, able to feel strongly, were given capacities on which the most favourable circumstances could make a strictly limited difference. Stephen could think scientifically, and she had a feeling and discriminating capacity. They could both throw off their clothes and make love. It didn't seem to be enough.

She said, 'He doesn't want a change of company. It isn't that he wants other women. It might be better if he did. I don't mean that. I'd hate it...When I was living in Paris,' she said in a conversational tone, 'Joseph was perfect to me. Without any reservations at all. And I wasn't especially agreeable. Not that there's any way of being agreeable, if you can't give back in equal measure.'

Perhaps in the eye of God, or whoever first spoke of

sowing and reaping, there was a weird sort of justice in it. Although, try as she would, she could not entirely think so: it was more like bad management than justice. All those people attached to the wrong people. In Paris, the balance went against Joseph. Now she knew what it felt like. Lessons, lessons. Except that in one respect he had been luckier—in being left with his work. When all else failed, there was the task. No wonder labour was so highly regarded!

'Anyway,' she said, suddenly brisk. 'We ought to disappear, darling Russell. I've got an appointment with Ken Simmons about the Bureau. He's negotiating with the other solicitor.'

Catching the waiter's eye, Russell felt for his wallet. 'Ignore everything I've said. When you remember how helpful I've been to everyone lately—I'm not in the strongest position to give advice. Stephen might be ill. I'd never notice.'

Zoe smiled, then stopped smiling so that she could apply her lipstick. 'Ill! He's well and strong, I'm glad to say.' She watched the waiter whip away the plate and the notes Russell had placed on it. 'Everything's all right. I've just discovered that nothing is what it seems. And there's no remedy for a discovery like that. Except to digest it. And a delicious lunch like this,' she added, as they rose from the padded leather banquette.

'I wasn't tactful,' Russell said.

Zoe smiled. 'I didn't tell many lies, either. The difference it makes! No wonder people get ill! You could develop rabies by suppressing what is and knowingly substituting what is not.'

'If we always act knowingly.'

They looked at each other with profound affection on the

deserted, curved, carpeted stairway leading up to the street.

'Oh, you too can deceive yourself in three easy lessons,' Zoe said carelessly.

•

The postman's whistle approached and withdrew tantalisingly up and down the steep suburban hills above the harbour. It danced into a cul-de-sac and was lost, silent for minutes, while a retired elderly gentleman provided a shady seat in the garden and a glass of lemonade. Guileless middle-aged widows sympathised with the Christmas burden slung over the postman's shoulder and offered cups of tea. Tough young matrons grabbed the mail from his hands without thanks, regarding politeness, charm, as something like capital, to be hoarded against a run on the banks. What looks like meanness is sometimes a lack of self-confidence, although quite often it is actually meanness.

Zoe waited. It was Lily's birthday, the day of her first dinner party since her 'retirement'. 'By popular demand,' she said, 'further personal appearances. And Russell's taking the afternoon off.'

Zoe had promised to help. Within hours of their decision to sell, the work of the Bureau had been taken over, and every day since then, during Stephen's absence in Melbourne and Canberra, she had loafed, enjoyed herself, swimming daily in the pool that had replaced her father's tennis court, meeting friends for lunch, visiting others for dinner, taking fruit and novels to another in hospital.

While she was in the presence of these diverse friends with whom she had shared moments of comprehension that were a kind of love, Zoe felt alive. The irreplaceable nature of each person touched her. Alone at home, in Stephen's world, though Stephen was absent, he overcame her. Her heart beat in trepidation. She sat motionless for hours. She wept bitterly. But sometimes she succeeded in holding that life at bay. Then, like a research worker she tracked hope from reference to reference and the path led straight to people. Those she cared about had qualities in common. With an access of joy, Zoe thought: there will always be people like this!

Though lovers be lost love shall not;
And death shall have no dominion.

And like someone in a fable, she marvelled at the landscape and its inhabitants and felt she had fallen among angels. Since she and Stephen had resolved to speak on his return, gifts had been mysteriously lavished on her—optimism, lightness of heart, something like grace.

In this new buoyant mood, she went up the path to wait for the postman before walking along the beach to Lily's place. A bunch of keys jingled in her hand: she had locked the house. A helicopter racketed by overhead.

'They've all remembered you today!' the postman announced, arriving at the gate. A fair, open-faced young man, he handed Zoe two parcels and a bundle of letters and cards.

They both smiled.

'Lighten your load,' Zoe said.

'Don't remind me of it!' He sagged at the knees, gave a wave, and made for the next house, sorting envelopes as he went.

Skimming back to the sealed-up house, muttering 'dimwit' at herself for having locked it, Zoe glanced at the parcels, left them on the hall table, and sifted through the cards and letters. One from Anna. Faintly surprised, she took this and others whose handwriting made her eyes widen with pleasure into the sitting room. There, she opened Anna's letter and read—at first swiftly, then with increasing slowness. Spreading from some place above and behind her ears, ice sheathed her scalp. Leaving doors flung open, she ran down through the garden, down the narrow tree-hung track to the beach, and ran and stumbled and ran along the beach to Russell.

Home from work, making himself useful, he had just replaced the globe in the lamp at the gate when he saw Zoe coming up the short hill. He waved and watched her for a few seconds, then went to meet her at the lower gate. She stared at him.

'What's happened?...Get your breath. You must have run all the way.' He touched her fingers.

She stared into his eyes, and saw that he knew nothing. There was only concern for her. His letter had not arrived yet. She took one of his hands in her left hand, and pressed it feverishly, as though he were very ill, and she distracted to know how to save him. Russell looked round the quiet street, deep in trees, then drew Zoe inside the garden and closed the big gates. She pushed the crumpled pages of her letter against his chest and turned away. 'It's Anna.'

•

Dear Zoe and Stephen,

There's no way of breaking it gently. I expect to be dead by the time you read this. Suicide is easy. All you have to do is not be found too soon. Russell and I have loved each other for a long time. I don't want to be alive without him any more. There has been too much unhappiness. I'm tired. It was never feasible for us to be happy at the expense of Lily and the girls. Everything must be at our expense, and everything has been.

The first thing I noticed about Russell was that he often felt another person's situation more profoundly than the person himself. As if he could see more. He could do this for everyone but me. I was too close. I'd seen so many miserable people handing out blows that I didn't want to be like them. I was too vain ever to put myself on their side. No one could say our intentions weren't good, self-sacrificing, and perhaps, in the end, wicked. Not to be together is worse than death. To be perpetually on the side of understanding and sacrifice is not only hard beyond bearing, but against some law of survival. Sometimes even we might have had the greater claim. It's ironic that this responsibility and thought for other which is usually regarded as 'good' should lead to death. Because this sort of death is not good. Therefore, good is bad. Or is it love that's bad? Or is it the denial of mutual love that leads to death, or death-in-life?

When you live alone, you have years of hours when you can lie on your bed and think. And when I was alone, waiting for him to arrive or to ring, I thought about him, trying to solve it in my mind. Then when I woke one day and understood that years had gone by in this way, I decided to make a change. You found out by accident, Zo, and I didn't care. I had some idea that I would ruin myself, do anything to kill the feeling. Anyone was welcome to help in the process.

The funny thing is, the worst part has been the surprise. In a way, I'm dying of surprise. It would never have occurred to me that it could end like this. I have written to Russell. Once or twice I tried to tell you something, but didn't. I love you both.

Anna

Russell held the solid double gates.

Shivering, Zoe glanced at his back, and sat down on a rock a few yards away, her collar pushed up to cover her cold neck, frozen hands pressed over her ears. The sun blazed down darkly, without heat.

Russell was pounding past her in the direction of the house, shouting to her to follow. She saw the soles of his shoes as she ran after him.

He was tearing at the telephone directory when she reached him.

'What? What?' she cried, and they looked at each other with blank eyes.

'That doctor she's staying with. What's her number? There's still time.'

'Enquiries. You'll have to ring the exchange.'

Russell rang enquiries. Zoe pushed a pad and pen towards him across the table. He rang the house of the woman doctor Anna had been visiting. A housekeeper told him that the doctor was at the local hospital. She gave him the number. Mrs Clermont had left for Sydney in her car early in the morning. He rang the hospital and waited.

'Oh, Zo, you're here!' Lily emerged from the kitchen and came down the hall. 'We're out of soda water. I forgot to order it. How do you like my hair? I went to that new man up the street. He can cut.' She turned to the big oval looking-glass. 'But he *prances* too much, and goes in for that badinage they learn from television comperes. So wearing!' Suddenly, as though a cold wind had encircled her, she glanced attentively at Zoe. 'Who's Russell ringing?'

Russell was introducing himself to the doctor, finally traced in some far corner of the hospital, as Anna Clermont's brother-in-law.

'That's stretching it,' Lily muttered.

Zoe was listening to him, watching him, watching Lily, as though her heart were a metronome. Talking, he saw the two women and with an oddly decisive gesture thrust the letter at

Zoe, indicating that she should give it to his wife.

'What on earth's going on? You look frightful! I didn't notice...What's the agitation?' Lily stared at Zoe, then at the letter in her hand. In a lower voice she asked, 'What's wrong with Anna?'

'Come in here.' Feeling doomed, a spreader of doom, without choice, Zoe led the way to the sitting room. 'He wants you to see this.' They stood facing each other on one of the beautiful worn rugs, surrounded by the chairs, sofas, small tables that had been her mother's pride.

'But Lily—' she hesitated. 'It's worse than anything you're expecting. *Not* anything about the girls. But expect something bad.'

In silence, the letter passed from her hand to Lily's. With a wondering look, in slow motion, unable to move her eyes from Zoe who knew, Lily sank in to one of the big armchairs.

A sort of superhuman alertness and clarity of mind descended on Zoe, as though she had received a message advising that even yet, if everyone acted with extreme composure and made no least mistake, even yet, death might be averted. She poured a large brandy and put the glass in Lily's free hand. 'Drink that.'

At the door to the hall, she heard Russell say, 'Thank you again. I'll let you know.'

He turned to her, thinking but not seeing.

'What?' Like someone at a great distance, she tried to attract his attention by raising an arm.

'She left this morning. Drove off in the car. In good

spirits, according to this woman. If she came home, she should be at her flat.' He dived at the telephone, dialling Anna's number. In her apartment the bell rang, and rang, and rang, emptily.

'Go there! Go and see!' Zoe said. 'I'd come too, but there's Lily, and in case there's news. But ring us as soon as you get there.'

Their eyes exchanged messages. Russell felt for his car keys. They both heard, at the distant gate, the postman's whistle.

'The letter,' he said, and made for the front door. Then he remembered and went past Zoe into the sitting room. He and Lily stared at each other. 'I'm going to look for her. I'm going to her flat. Zo's staying here.'

Seeming not to hear, Lily looked down and balanced her empty glass lightly between her fingers. Zoe went to what used to be her father's study and from there, leaving the telephone in the hall for incoming messages, rang to put off the evening's guests. Lily had eaten out at some new place the night before, she said, and was laid low with food poisoning. Yes, what a pity on her birthday! Apologising for the postponement of the dinner, accepting sympathy for Lily with the skill of a consummate liar, she carved some lines in the soft wood of the desk with a long thumbnail. She pressed her fingers so hard against her forehead that small blotches appeared on the white skin when she took her hand away. That left Tom, who had written to ask Anna to marry him.

In the hall, the telephone rang. Skidding out to answer it,

she bumped into the doorframe clumsily. Lily appeared at the top of the stairs when she had her hand on the receiver and prompted her with a series of tiny nods.

It was Russell. 'The flat's empty, but there's fresh food in the fridge—milk, chicken, cheese. There's fruit in a bowl, and flowers.'

'Then—what does that mean?' Zoe asked vacantly.

'I wish to God I knew. I suppose someone might have opened the place up to welcome her back. They might have got this stuff in and spread the flowers about.'

'We should have done that,' Zoe cried.

'No messages?'

'Nothing. Dead silence.' She amended, 'Nothing. The phone hasn't rung. What are you going to do? Was there a letter for you?'

'Yes. I'll leave a note for anyone who comes in, asking them to call us. We'll have to notify the police.'

'Oh. Is that necessary?' Zoe asked in a small voice. If you agreed to think it might be all over, it might be all over. 'Is that wise?' she murmured, afraid of being overheard.

'I don't know what's wise,' he said with simple helplessness. 'Is Lily all right? When will Stephen be in?'

'Lily's okay.' She glanced at her watch, but was unable to understand it. At length she said, 'Soon. He'll be in soon. Anna was supposed to collect him.'

Lily had come quietly downstairs and was almost beside her when she replaced the receiver on the stand. 'I looked through a pile of photographs and found a few of Anna. For

217

the police,' she added, as she passed the thin wad to Zoe.

Unnerved by Lily's calm and appalling forethought, by the cold squares of paper, Zoe trembled unobtrusively, and closed her teeth together. She said conversationally, 'I haven't put Tom off yet.'

The two women stood waiting and listening. 'I'm going to make some coffee and sandwiches,' said the one whose house this now was.

'Are you?' Zoe was surprised, but people had to occupy themselves. 'I'll help.' Yet she remained suspended attentively on the spot, swaying on her feet.

'Did you know?' Lily stood quite turned away from her, like someone miming suffering and reticence and shock.

'No. I knew nothing. I knew nothing.' With sudden intensity she disclaimed any part in a conspiracy.

Lily listened with head bent, breathing through her mouth, nervously touching her parted lips, then having heard, went straight to the kitchen, where she and Zoe made themselves resourceful in the matter of sandwich fillings.

Half an hour later the front door crashed open and they ran to meet Russell. 'Any news?'

'I rang the police from her flat,' he said.

Zoe told him, 'I haven't put Tom off yet. I suppose he ought to know.'

Haggardly, Russell's eyes turned from his wife, from his sister, to the telephone.

'You wished him luck,' Zoe said in a hard voice, and instantly went to his side, putting an arm round his waist and leaning her face against him.

'No,' he said, gently releasing her.

'You only told me that?' she asked, almost joyfully, tears coming to her eyes, and Russell slid a hand across her shoulders.

Moving away, he said, 'They wanted the number of her car. They asked me to describe her. Someone's coming round to collect the letters and some photographs.'

'Lily thought of that. She found some.'

They walked about from room to room, passing and re-passing each other. Once, when Russell approached her, Lily said, 'It's the end, isn't it? Whatever happens.'

'It's the end.'

For no reason, she gave him her hand, and they stood like two strangers taking a formal farewell.

Zoe rang Tom and urged him to go home to look for a note from Anna. After that, he was to come immediately to Russell's house. She told him nothing else.

The police car pulled up and two huge men disappeared into the study with Russell. They asked questions, read and confiscated the letters, looked at Anna's living face, made non-committal remarks and went away.

Carrying in a tray from the kitchen, Zoe heard Russell reporting on their visit. Lily poured and distributed the coffee. 'I'd forgotten about it.'

'She might have stopped the car at any point on the way,' Russell said. 'There are bush tracks and old roads leading off the highway everywhere. If she left the car out of sight and then walked away…' The telephone rang and he ran to answer it. 'It's Stephen, Zo. You talk to him.'

'So early!' she said in amazement, then glanced at her watch and saw it was quite late.

In the cosy dark angle of the stairs the black telephone on its table and the comfortable upholstered chair waited. Zoe drew near it with a sort of horror, superstitiously convinced that the spreading of the news about Anna made its reversal less and less possible.

'Stephen…Darling…'

'I can scarcely hear you,' Stephen shouted. 'I'm still at the station. It's like an echo chamber. There's a fearful racket going on. This is the *fifth* phone I've tried. All the others have had their guts ripped out by teenage morons.'

'Stephen, *listen*. Come home straight away. To Russell's, I mean. Something's happened to Anna.'

'What?' he shouted. 'This is a bloody awful connection. You'll have to listen to me, if you can hear. We're late because Anna read the departures indicator instead of the arrivals and went to the wrong platform. Not like her. Then I waited and eventually she turned up. Then, being helpful, as we were getting into the car, she lifted my briefcase and some ring she wears snapped and broke. We found the metal part, but the stone's missing and Anna's out there now in the traffic, getting run over, searching around in the gravel for the chip of ruby or whatever it is. Are you listening?…Can you hear me?'

Circle on circle of surprise rose and expanded in Zoe till

she was only astonishment and relief listening to sounds through a black machine.

She shouted, 'Is Anna *there?*'

'I can hear when you raise your voice. We're late. That's why I'm ringing. She's a couple of hundred yards away, scrabbling round in the gravel at the risk of her life. I wish I'd got a taxi instead of arranging all this.'

Zoe wiped her eyes and cheeks with her bare hand and tried to stop crying. 'I know what ring it is.'

'I can't hear you.'

'It's the line. Get Anna and come home. Make her drive slowly.'

'Is anything wrong?'

'Everything's fine.' She continued to smear tears over her cheeks.

Aware that the others had come to listen, she spun round and jumped from the chair as the call ended. 'She's alive! She's alive, Russell! The letters must have been a mistake. She's with Stephen. They're on their way home.'

Russell leaned back against the wall with his eyes closed. Lily watched him. And while extraordinary changes were taking place in the souls of the two she left behind, Zoe searched down the side of the sofa for her handkerchief, still crying. And when she found it, she sat in a chair and cried for people, and the things that happen, and the way there seems to be no help for it.

'Stop, Zo!' It was Lily. 'I've made more coffee, and we'd better all have some and eat those sandwiches. But go and wash your face first, then come down. Use my powder, or anything you want.'

When she returned minutes later, Lily was alone, eating and drinking. 'I didn't wait. I was suddenly ravenous. The condemned man...'

Zoe confessed, 'So am I,' and helping herself, plumped down in a chair, carefully balancing cup and plate in either hand. She felt bruised all over. 'Well then, what next, Lily?' she asked without diplomacy, when she had demolished a bacon and cream cheese sandwich.

'That's a question! One of the announcements tonight was about going off to London for a year. I want to finish my thesis. I was going to pick up my work, and be within reach of the girls. I wouldn't smother them now. So it seems I can live without Russell. Anna thought she couldn't.'

'Was Russell going, too?'

'There are people he'd like to see. He sets great store by his friends, as you know.'

Avoiding her eyes, Zoe reached across to the table for another sandwich, then offered the plate to Lily.

'He's involved in too many things to go suddenly. He knows no one's indispensable, but the idea was that I should have the time to myself to work, and see my sisters, and the girls.'

'I see. Then—but what about Russell? Were you—in effect—leaving him?'

'No, of course not.' Lily covered her face with her hands.

Just then Tom came in with Russell. 'What was the panic,

Zo? Russell says they're on the way from the station. Greetings, anyway. I'm early for dinner, but just in time for a drink.'

'Oh, the panic?' To keep him at a distance from Lily, Zoe went over to him, smiling. 'That was in case Anna forgot to go to the station. But would you be a great help now that you're lured over early? Lily and I are busy in the kitchen, and Russell has to see Stephen the minute he arrives. *Could* you go along to the shops at the junction—the second junction—to get a few things?'

Tom displayed fortitude and agreed to go. Zoe extracted Lily from the spotlight, saying that they would have to make out the list in the kitchen. There, they quickly composed Tom's task. Promised lavish drinks and rewards on his return, Tom was ushered to the door and directed to travel on a small back road to avoid the city traffic.

'Rotten way to treat him, but we had to get rid of him before they arrive.' Zoe looked round. 'It's my fault that he's here at all. But I thought he might have had a message.'

They drifted inside again. Russell wound up the clock. Zoe drank some coffee and finished her sandwich. Lily went upstairs to comb her hair. The doorbell rang as she came down again, and she answered it.

'Happy birthday! Many happy returns of the day!' Anna presented her with a parcel, which she accepted unsmiling, saying nothing.

Surprised, Anna returned her unreadable look. Inside, there were restrained but strange embraces, and the welcoming party seemed disinclined to speak. As the incomprehensibly intense expressions on the waiting faces struck the two new-comers, they glanced at each other.

Stephen said, 'She found the ring. The stone that was lost. Without even damaging her stockings.'

To the watchers, Anna appeared almost to glitter, her expression to flicker under the pressure of some about-to-be-revealed declaration. She was wearing a bare, simple, expensive black dress, a heavy silver bracelet. 'It clicked on to the floor of the car as we climbed in. We'd given up. I was so relieved. We'd crawled all over Central Station and the parking lot on our hands and knees. Stephen was patient.'

Everyone still watched her with peculiar vigilance. No one else could be looked at.

Lily asked, 'What ring is it, Anna?'

'Oh,' her frankness seemed at an end. 'It's nothing. Just a toy. Very fragile. That's why it broke so easily. I very seldom wear it.' She added, 'I've put it away.'

'Years ago,' Zoe said in a level voice, 'the first Christmas we all met, Anna and Russell pulled a cracker and the ring fell out. Russell gave it to her.' She received a great look of aston-ishment with compassion, saying, 'Oh, Anna!'

'Yes, it is that ring.' Anna looked down with an appearance of unconcern. 'It was a happy Christmas, and I'm sentimental about it. So there!' Her face bright and unclouded, she gazed at the company with a certain gaiety.

Stephen said, 'The air-conditioning broke down in the train. Are we going home to change, Zo, or did you bring everything with you? Why did we have to come straight here?

All I want is a shower.'

'I don't know.' Zoe took his hand pleadingly while he looked at her in mystification.

Anna glanced about. 'Is something wrong? I have a feeling we should go out and make another entrance. You're all standing there like—a jury. Executioners.'

'We do seem to have caused a funereal silence.'

Russell went to her side. 'Anna, I want you to come out with me. We'll go somewhere in the car. I'll explain when we're on the way.'

Her eyes read his face. She cast a wide, half-comprehending glance over the other assembled faces. 'Why? What's happened?'

'You'd better go with him,' Lily came in harshly. 'He and Zoe had letters from you this afternoon. What sort of a hoax was it? Till Stephen rang from Central, we thought you were dead.'

In the following uproar, only Anna was silent, only she remained still. Her mouth opened slightly with shock. Her colour faded and she had the appearance of someone alone thinking intricately and deeply. When at last she attended again to the company, she saw there were too many people. Then she left the room and the house and went up the path to her car.

Everyone, even Lily, exclaimed. She could not be allowed to hurl herself away from them. But Russell had followed without waiting for advice, and had overtaken her. Within seconds, the car moved off.

•

Upstairs, in her old bedroom, Zoe faced her husband. The two policemen had returned for further details about the supposed suicide; had been assured that she was now alive; had given up the letters (copies of which were held at their station); and declared that the missing person must appear before them within twenty-four hours so that it could be ascertained officially that she was not, in fact, dead by her own hand.

Tom had barged in, harassed and laden with his miscellaneous items of shopping, overheard the dialogue at the door between Stephen and the policemen, and now sat downstairs drinking steadily and eyeing an emerald ring he had bought on the off chance.

'All that time they've loved each other,' Zoe said. 'What a waste! The news that Anna isn't lying dead in the bush somewhere hasn't got through to me properly. I don't know how you feel. I could hardly feel worse if she *were* dead.'

'I don't feel so hot, either. In fact, I'm bloody freezing. And in the train I thought I'd never be cool again.'

'Have that shower. Warm you up.'

Stephen had read Anna's letter and, almost with disbelief, Zoe had seen him tremble. Since then they had spoken little, existing in a state of torpor. Opening his suitcase, he pulled out from a melange of clothing a clean shirt and socks and pants. 'For years I've thought she was all right,' he muttered angrily. 'She's wasted her whole life on this obsession. When David was alive she had plans to do something with her life.

Rotting away in that flat.'

Now, Zoe gave a humourless smile. 'That goes for all of us. But women are peculiar—like men—so their plans don't work out. Anyway, she's not twenty, but she's not dead, either. Aren't you sorry about them?' she asked carefully.

'I'm sorry for all three. But what was the matter with Russell? You only had to look at him! I'm going to have a shower.'

'Yes. He loves her.' Something old-fashioned like honour or duty had ruined their lives. What they had in common created love and also frustrated it. Still, Zoe thought cynically, if one thing didn't ruin your life, something else did. So perhaps it didn't matter. Leaning on her elbow across the bed, she watched Stephen, her heart beating slowly.

Downstairs, Tom could be heard—awake, but not sober, which was possibly a merciful thing, too.

'You're a very unusual woman, if I may say so. I admire the way you've taken this thing. I've always admired—*women*— with trained minds. And I've heard from certain people—not mentioning any names—but certain people have told me you're a remarkable woman.'

Interrupting, sitting on the arm of Lily's chair, Zoe asked, 'Am I interrupting?'

Lily turned up her eyes expressively. 'Do.'

'Back in a minute.' Tom unsteadily juggled his glass down on the table and left the room.

'Get a taxi and have him removed, for God's sake!' Lily begged her. 'I've had enough.'

Zoe came back from the telephone. 'Here in a second.'

'I was upstairs wandering about, then I came down to move the dishes and woke him. Alas! Don't *you* go. I don't want to be alone when they come back. If they come back.'

'No, we'll stay. Stephen's having a shower.' Zoe stacked cups and saucers on the tray and collected discarded sandwiches with small scallops eaten out of them. Comfort, common sense, sympathy, alliances were impossible; pretending that nothing had happened, noisy distractions, equally so. You could only be present and not add to the general distress by being unreal; only perform practical chores; only care.

'What a mess! What a mess!' Lily said sickly, as Tom came back into the room, looking damp about the face and hair.

A taxi tooted its horn at the gate.

'That's for you, Tom. We knew you wouldn't want to take your own car.'

Bemused, Tom nodded his small Chinese-looking head.

'We'll talk to you tomorrow. Thank you for all you've done. Ring before you come for the car, in case we're out.' Lily guided him up the steps. Zoe gave his address to the driver.

'You shunted him off home?' Stephen eyed them with interest a few minutes later. 'That was a bit rough.'

Censured, the women looked at each other. *Was* it rough? Neither of them felt able to tell. They returned Stephen's gaze as though he still possessed some faculty lost to them.

'It isn't appropriate to have semi-strangers around,' Lily explained.

'He was drunk,' Zoe added. 'Lily's under enough strain.

Everyone's tattered. Why should all this be paraded for his benefit? It's none of his business.'

Stephen pulled an unpleasant face. 'He only wanted to marry her.'

'He's surely had his answer?'

Holding her head, Lily said, 'Stop quarrelling, you two!'

There was instantaneous silence. Zoe closed her eyes in compunction. Stephen ate some olives from a dish near his hand, and from under their eyebrows, heads lowered a little as if pressed down by too-dazzling sunlight, he and Zoe looked into each other deeply. They both said, 'Sorry, Lily,' and Stephen asked, 'Would you like a drink?'

So they sat in silence, drinking and waiting, till the absent ones returned.

•

'What did Lily mean,' Stephen asked as they entered their own house, switching on lights, 'when she said we had troubles of our own?'

'Don't you know?' Zoe looked at him at chest level, studying the small flowers on his imported tie.

'Should I?' Bags and briefcases seemed to be hanging all over him. His glasses had slipped down his nose. They had come home in Anna's car: Anna was to be driven over later to stay with them.

'You look like a walking luggage rack. You must be famished.'

'Lily kept promising food, then forgetting. Is she sorry for you?'

'Both of us, I suppose. While you're getting rid of that stuff, I'll organise some dinner.'

Before they sat down to eat, Stephen appeared silently beside her in the kitchen, complaining of his enforced absence in Melbourne and Canberra. Zoe leaned against him with a sad, divided pleasure. Whatever the textbooks said, lovers who shared beds and each other with considerable satisfaction frequently parted forever in the morning. Because, because, she thought. Because they were human. And more complicated even than that.

They sat across the table from each other, Stephen pouring the wine, and Zoe serving a casserole she had prepared the previous evening. 'We should be celebrating Lily's birthday now.' She was still wearing the dark-blue shirt and slacks she had put on years ago, in the morning. 'Tell me something different. Not about all this.'

'Does it have to be cheerful?'

'It would help.'

But sooner or later, every attempt to exchange the details of their separation—meetings with common friends—led back to today, to the three in the old Howard house along the beach. The cats came in from the verandah providing light relief, displaying composure, attending with grape-green eyes. They strolled about like feted courtesans.

Stephen said, with mixed venom and amusement, eating vigorously, and glancing up at her over his plate, 'Lily's not in much of a position to be sorry for us, is she?'

With an effort of will, Zoe met his eyes. 'Would you like more of this, or some salad?' He could deride Lily in this situation without surprising her. He felt free to say anything. Because of this, he could always end discussions and win arguments.

An extraordinary nausea swept over Zoe at the thought of their life. And everything her eye touched was part of the nausea. Like a traitor whose ways had on an instant become abhorrent to her, she glanced about, opening her hands wide with revulsion to drop secrets, weapons.

'Salad, thanks. What's the matter?'

Supplicating, Zoe said, 'I know you hate melodrama. Everything ought to be neat and manageable, especially the way we all feel, but it isn't. You've read Anna's letter. You've noticed that Lily feels sorry for us.' She pleaded, 'If there's something in particular you don't like about the way we live, we can change it. We're free, in a way. We're here in a temporarily peaceful, prosperous place. But nothing's certain. People die every day. We haven't got time to brood our lives away. And we don't have to.

'If there's something about me that's killing you off, say so. I'll go away. We seem to exist for the purpose of concealing ourselves from each other. It's as if you only lived to suppress me—as if I were a fire out of control. It doesn't seem very constructive. If this is the only satisfaction I can give you apart from sex, it isn't enough. And it isn't the sort of satisfaction I feel allowed to go on giving. What do you hold against me, apart from the fact that I've loved you?'

Under the power of this involuntary cry, with its compelling force, they stared at each other, each appearing magnified and infinitely strange in the other's sight.

'Or is that it?' she said slowly.

'It could be that,' Stephen answered, with a fixed listening look.

Like someone kidnapped and dragged across a frontier into a place where the language and the laws were wholly unknown, he glanced about with a mixture of desperation and bafflement. They both sat in active, anguished silence, like accident victims retracing events that led always to the same crash and destruction. As though they could not escape from the accident, the physical suffering continued. They were bodies tossed over and over on a highway. Their faces were haggard.

At last Stephen found something to offer. 'That time I'd been ill and you had to go to the office for a couple of days, I went up to the attic to see if there were any leaks in the roof. I saw your press-cutting books. I read your letters from Joseph.'

'You read the letters? Did you, *really*?' So at odds with her knowledge of him! An angry, intimidating man, but a man crammed with rigid, erratic ideas of 'the right thing'. Zoe shook her head, trying to believe him.

'If I was inquisitive enough to do that, I should remember what I thought, but I don't. Do you think I was jealous?'

They gazed at each other, not moving their eyes more than fractionally to explore another part of the eyes opposite. These long looks nourished their hearts, as if their eyes knew everything that mattered.

'Jealous? Why should you be? How could you be?'

In his eyes there was a change. Zoe now saw resentment, dislike, violent hatred. 'Don't look at me like that. It doesn't matter about the letters. Why be like this?'

'Because I'm difficult?' he suggested. 'I have trouble with myself. I don't always know what I feel. You can't understand that.'

'No, but I believe that you often don't. Once, I couldn't.' That it might be in a way less exacting to be like Stephen occurred to Zoe. Jealous in her turn, she thought: what a lot you can get away with when you don't know what you're doing! 'Is it my fault?'

'I'd never have married anyone else.'

'It hasn't been a raving success.'

A total and exact reciprocation of feeling happened occasionally in real life, and often in children's tales, but more often still the exalted expectation led straight to unhappiness and death. What choice was there but to give what you had without bargaining? Her early attachment to justice had done her a disservice: a kind of justice did exist, but there were times when one or two things mattered more.

'Is it so bad if I'd like your life to please you? A blind man could see that it doesn't. You make me feel it. Then I'm unpleasant to someone else. It's kinder to the entire world to take some notice of your own preferences. Unless'—she looked up suddenly—'this life *is* your preference?'

Amazing her, he said, 'I've been satisfied. I thought you were satisfied. We make out better than most, I thought. And no shortage of work or play.'

'But if none of it was giving you any pleasure. If everything was a sort of duty to you. This grudge...' Her, the world, himself? His eyes were uncomprehending. Cold, at an astronomical distance, his eyes made her feel. Grudge? Grudge?

'You seem to *bear* your life instead of living it.' From the beginning he had sworn he would never willingly share her attention with children. Later, the prospect of children being used as restoratives for an ailing partnership was abhorrent to her. Journeys abroad, alone or together, had been rejected. There was too much work; he was too busy, he always said.

Pressing her eyes shut with her fingers, Zoe saw a myriad geometrical shapes symmetrical as snowflakes magnified. 'I've cried so much today...I think you've wanted circumstances always to confirm your reasons for melancholy. Because you've been used all your life to thinking of yourself as ill-treated. Maligned. Neglected. With reason, till I appeared. I threatened you. Threatened to lose that person who's never been lucky, the one you knew best. You're afraid of me. Because you might have loved me and had to change your ideas. And the funny thing is—if it strikes you as funny—I'm afraid of you.'

All of Stephen's senses listened as though to the voice of an oracle. What Zoe so dispassionately said, without reflection or hesitation, had the authority of absolute truth. At the french windows, hands in pockets, he stared out at the black space that was the harbour, at the scattered lights of houses across the bay. Church bells were pealing in the distance. Zoe looked at his back. She cared about him, but she felt his so-familiar silence, his satisfaction with their prison, his waiting on her initiative, the silent presentation of himself as a challenge, as so many crimes. The obsessiveness with which he worked, the pervasiveness of his pessimism, were crimes. She thought: I cannot solve you. You must solve yourself.

Outside, there were footsteps along the verandah and Anna appeared in the open doorway, still dressed for the party, made-up, scented, breathing.

'Just in time for dinner!' Stephen said.

'Come inside, Anna.' Zoe looked at her, at the brother and sister together, temperamentally so dissimilar, sharing nothing but their parents and the colour of their eyes.

'Russell drove me over. I promised to stay here tonight, but let's not talk. There's been so much of it.' She sighed, dropped her bag, put a hand to her head, and fainted for the first time in her life.

•

As she cooked breakfast and set out plates, Zoe glanced through the open door to Anna and Stephen on the verandah. Anna had washed her hair in the shower before coming down. The wet strands dampening the seaweed green of her cotton sweater, borrowed from Zoe, made her look like a mermaid. She had volunteered nothing. Stephen had valiantly tried five or six subjects of an impersonal nature, but each had proved unsafe in its turn. Anna looked through him. Sympathetically, Zoe caught his eye. He said to his sister, 'Zo thinks you won't be interested.'

'I am,' she insisted courteously, then added honestly, 'and I'm not. My mind's a bit foggy this morning.'

At a sign from Zoe, they came in to eat breakfast.

Holding her glass of orange juice, Anna said, 'What do I say? "I'm sorry I accidentally posted suicide notes written years ago"? That's what happened. Then—it's too complicated to say how—having realised it was necessary to kill myself, I realised it was necessary not to. I kept those letters as a—because too much was invested in them of someone worth more than I am, to throw them away. They were in a drawer. I wrote my Christmas cards and stamped them and put them in the same place, till it was time to post them. When I was leaving on my travels I stuffed them all in a basket, intending to post them somewhere along the way.' She said, 'I'm very sorry.'

'Eat up,' Zoe said after a brief pause, so the three of them began to, with considerable appetite.

Anna finished her slice of toast and honey, and drank some coffee. 'That was the easy way out last night—fainting. But it's impossible to convey how—thinking you'd learned to live with what was given—how so unexpectedly you turn into a suicidal person. It's as surprising as waking up and finding you'd turned into an African or a Chinese. And you can never quite be what you were before. You do forget, though,' she added with more animation, 'but now I've made it public property forgetting's going to be harder.'

Stephen said, 'I suppose everyone thinks about it at some time.'

'Do they?' She was surprised. 'I never did.'

'Not when we were young, when we lived with them?'

'*No*,' she said strongly. 'Why should people like that make me want to die? I wanted to live more than ever when I saw them. *They* couldn't influence me out of existence.' In the indignant glance, a younger Anna was visible and Stephen smiled.

'*I* thought of it.'

Her eyes opened wider, moved thoughtfully over the sunny breakfast table. 'No, I've always been convinced that if you're of sound mind you have no real right to—lower the confidence of the world. Something like that. By deserting it. Letting it be known that you reject what makes everyone else cling to life. Yet one morning I woke up and my mind was still sound but suicide had chosen me. And none of my previous convictions had any weight at all. It had seductive arguments. I argued back as if only the promise that death was instantly available made it possible—as if my arguments had to be completed before I could go. I know it sounds confused.'

The refrigerator hummed. Outside, there were distant sounds of traffic and close at hand a peewit warbled loudly.

'And in the end?' Zoe ventured to ask.

'Oh, in the end'—Anna propped an elbow on the table and shaded her eyes from the sun—'a different thought came into my mind. A new idea occurred to me. I made a choice. I ate a very stale piece of apple pie—about the only food I had in the house. When I picked it up, after having thought the great thought, I saw that I was going to stay alive. By that time, it almost felt as if I'd gone already, leaving my body to follow with the luggage. So it was all—rather complex—at the time,' she finished obscurely.

'Did anybody know?' Stephen asked.

She shook her head. 'Nobody said. I had insisted to the point of death. Like a battle between myself and something so large that you'd have to call it God or Necessity. The will of the world.'

She paused again, supporting her forehead against the fingers of both hands. 'I did say "Help!" to a few people, because I resisted the idea of killing myself. But it was an experience that would confirm your belief that there's still a great deal to be discovered about—not only human nature, but—I don't know how to describe it—psychic phenomena, extrasensory perception. I'd heard of sick animals being hunted and killed by others, but I hadn't realised what it meant till then. I was frightened. I saw that it was a very risky thing ever to let it be known that you were weak and close to death. It was like pressing against a wall as deep as eternity, with your loved ones turned to murderous enemies, or at best indifferent acquaintances.'

Stephen and Zoe exchanged glances. 'Us, too?' she asked.

'You had your own problems,' Anna said, lifting her head so that her face was visible, amazing them by her tranquillity. 'You could feel it was a natural law. The hostility, and fault-finding. I was drowning and wanted to help to live; everyone seemed bent on giving me help to drown. The experience, which I can't describe, of picking yourself up while you're under attack is like a long, ghastly course in self-reliance, like trying to survive a civil war with everyone you care about on the opposite side. Bitter animosity. All so out of proportion. I realised after numerous rather agonising shocks that we were all on strange ground, if I make myself clear, and I'm sure I don't.' She sat back in her chair answering the serious looks of her listeners with an air of repose.

Stephen could not refrain from saying, 'It was all your own state of mind.'

'Well,' Anna said, then paused. 'Even at the time, I knew that would be an accusation. It's only—that when you're close to death, everything wears a look of eternity. Ephemeral expressions of bad feeling felt to me'—she clapped a hand to her chest—'like a last message from the human race. The terrible urgency, and the way no one could hear. You're like a wireless receiver tuned to finer and finer degrees of receptivity, so that you receive messages other people aren't really aware of sending.'

Zoe stared through the window at the pattern of branches against some puffy white clouds, newly arrived. 'I can imagine what you mean.'

Anna said, 'But it was so long ago. Years ago. I'm another person. I'm telling you this because I owe it to you, after yesterday. But it's ancient history. It's a story about someone else.'

'Was it after this,' Zoe asked suddenly, remembering, 'that you left the gallery and took up your work?'

'Twenty-four hours a day. No wonder I made progress! I

learned to live in the moment.' Looking back, she half-laughed.

'But is it truly like a story about someone else, Anna? Stephen saw you at Ten Mile Beach. He said you were very unhappy, and that's since Canada.'

'Oh.' Gravely, she appeared to think about that day. She looked at them both with unsmiling eyes for a time. 'No, it wasn't like that. I hadn't been home very long. Russell and I were going for a walk. You confiscated him, Zo, and he had to go or refuse noticeably. But being deprived of his company meant so much less than it would have once, that I was—sad. And then (I know it sounds contradictory), I had forgotten what his presence was like. And although the walk didn't matter, Russell did. More or less eternally. So there you are. All told, if not explained.'

'Why should it be?' Zoe looked at her with a sombre shame. 'You needn't have felt...It wasn't necessary...'

Abruptly, frowning at her, Stephen asked, 'What's happening about you and Russell?'

From the front of the house, Russell called, 'Hullo! Anyone out of bed?' Anna was stared at. As though by choice, she left her face undefended, and her trustfulness was felt by the others as a gift of purest generosity, as a sort of honour. Expectant, they met her eyes, watched her rise and go from the room.

Stephen went outside to contemplate the view. Left alone in the kitchen, Zoe cleared away the dishes. It occurred to her that there might be nothing braver in the world than to allow yourself to be understood.

•

Russell and Anna were in the sitting room.

Mrs Trent had arrived and was ironing and listening to the transistor.

At Stephen's invitation, Zoe had gone to join him outside. They walked down to the wall near the track and sat there.

'Zo...' Stephen cleared his throat. Hands pressed to the stone on either side of him, he stared at the lawn. 'I wanted to say—don't talk about leaving me. You wouldn't, would you? Even if you hated me. You'd be so sorry for me for having lost what I'd lost that you'd never let me guess.'

Abstractedly, she pulled a weed from the garden beside her. 'I'm so bad at hating.'

'You won't leave me, then?'

'I don't know. I might have to.'

'Because I'm an impossible task, and don't always treat you—as I should.'

Heavy-eyed, she gazed at him, and laid the frail weed on his thigh. She was tired of avowing love to scepticism, disbelief and fear. 'I've heard better reasons for living with someone.'

'You couldn't think I mightn't have been worth the effort, or you'd have wasted your life.'

She gave a short, incredulous laugh. 'When did you think of all this?'

'Last night.' Intent on his private agenda, Stephen went on, 'And at the beginning, there were good years.'

'Oh, yes,' she agreed, without belief, unable to remember.

'But perhaps it was never right.'

Picking up the weed and twirling it between his fingers, he said, 'Well, it went wrong. I helped it. One thing—as you discovered for me last night—I couldn't part with the past. And I'd never loved anyone before. I'm not good at it. It isn't easy to change. I thought you regretted what you'd given up. And then, when we got married, I'd stayed on in that job and saved with the idea of going back to university full-time.'

'For God's sake!' Zoe looked at him with stupefaction. 'You wouldn't have thought of telling me?'

'I hadn't told anyone.'

'I'm not *anyone*.' She stared at him furiously. 'What were you going to do?'

'Research.'

'What? In chemistry? Medicine?'

He nodded, and they were silent. Zoe saw this was exactly the sort of work he would have excelled in. 'Just tell me why,' she said hopelessly, at length. 'Was it so that you could blame me? So that you'd have something to resent from the beginning? You were able to blame me without having to make the effort to take the initiative for your own life, weren't you?'

With a bleak look of self-knowledge, a new expression on Stephen's face, he turned to Zoe and said, 'Yes.' He paused. 'It isn't reasonable, but later—I blamed you for not having forced something better on me than the press. If you want admissions, there's one for you. Russell's political. He's never had to be interested in the press as a business. It's had another purpose altogether for him—printing stuff cheaply, the paper, holding

242

meetings, finding jobs. How the country works or doesn't work, having an influence—that's Russell's life.

'At the same time, he's had enough—I suppose, personal magnetism, to attract and keep such a good bunch of workers as permanent staff that we've made money hand over fist.' He added, with unusual diffidence, 'But, as we know, even that's only one side of him. It isn't healthy to find yourself constantly compared with someone like Russell.'

'Oh.' Zoe saw, and the seeing was like a long fall in space. Russell was a complex and subtle man whose lifestyle had so strong an effect on acquaintances that those who were less than dedicated to their own qualities frequently felt there was no other way of being than his. All his life he had tested himself mentally and physically. He worked harder at a great variety of tasks and accomplished more than most people, and this, with apparent ease. Whatever he did, he did very well indeed.

Stephen said, 'It's paralysing to feel yourself found wanting daily. Your abilities don't measure up. You stop trying. Especially when you aren't doing the work you would choose. In spite of what he thinks, it isn't what he does, it's what he is that matters. The fact remains…'

'How awful if you've felt yourself in competition! Who said we all had to be like Russell? He's no hypocrite. He knows himself. But he certainly doesn't consider himself the measure of all things. He has a tremendously high opinion of you.'

'I know. But there the comparison was. It's had a bad effect. On Lily, too, quite possibly. It's a—I suppose it's a spiritual superiority. Not only temperament and abilities. You should understand that.'

Zoe watched this fluent, rational Stephen, who looked as though he never made guests uncomfortable with his sarcasm, never shattered her confidence, employed verbal terrorist tactics with the skill of a trained provocateur.

'Why didn't you ever speak?' she asked. 'Plenty of sadness can't be avoided. This was unnecessary.'

Hunching forward over his knees, Stephen pushed his hands through his wiry hair. 'I didn't face it. You've never threatened to leave me. Two other people tell me we have problems of our own. Rude awakening. I was in the habit of putting up with things all my life.' He seemed dazed.

Out of touch, Zoe thought, understanding that to be out of touch with people was natural to him. He was not naturally intuitive. This natural way of his was the cause of so many incidents that had left scars across sore places in her being.

'Anyway,' she said, turning to look round the garden, to breathe, 'you know quite well that Russell's detested as much as he's admired.'

Stephen smiled. 'But look who they are. Paranoids. Nature's Nazis.'

She nodded. 'True. So what happens now? Dispose of your half of the press, and do what you wanted to do years ago?'

'I think so. We'll probably have to arrange a few riots and demonstrations in favour of my admission—at this age.' Saying 'we', he looked at her.

'Nothing could be easier,' Zoe assured him. 'Riots of all types and sizes catered for.'

'If you can't expect first-class work from a brain as old as this, still I'll do something worthwhile.'

'Don't. Don't be so humble.' She took his arm between hers and held it, and they sat in silence for a time.

'You,' Stephen said, looking into her face, at the silvery pallor of her skin. 'What will you do? I wondered if you'd like to go back to film work? The situation's changing here, according to the papers.'

Zoe smiled at the tidiness of the idea that they should both return to abandoned careers. Some things really die. Her interest had really died. He had really killed her enthusiasm. He had no conception of the damage he had done. Lucky Stephen! It was not even, any more, any of his affair, this damage he had given her. 'I'd have to think. I mean—I'll have to think.'

Sounding decisive, her expression open and pleased, Zoe was inwardly aghast to feel the facility she had achieved in counterfeiting. I could make myself do anything, she thought. I have become a dangerous person. She would now make an excellent actress, or confidence trickster, or prostitute, she reflected, and remembered reading in some hairdresser's magazine that many women imagined this of themselves. The difference was that Zoe felt her genius to lie in her powers of deception. And once, and once, she had not been like that.

She said, 'I feel like a lion tamer and his lion, both. And the lion's been ill-treated—by me. I've forced myself to behave differently from the way I've felt. Like bending a steel bar with my will. Now comes the backlash. Now comes the palace revolution. I'm glad about everything, but I don't care. I do care about Russell and Anna, but—'

But as for herself and Stephen, perhaps there simply were no marriages of the sort she envisaged. Happy ones. It was often suggested these days that the institution would have to change or go. Perhaps Russell's 'You're always going to have to make allowances' was what everybody did all the time. In which case, what a pity! So much pitiful dissembling.

'Do you think there's nobody who's much good?' she asked Stephen in tones of exhaustion. 'Do you think if you knew anyone well enough you'd come on doors marked—cruel things? Has everyone got—weird moods and unaccountability hidden away behind nice faces? What I really mean is—is there perhaps some small thing that's radically wrong with everyone? We fall into obsessions without wanting to. Anna says she's always despised women who've behaved as she's behaved. Russell acted from the highest motives and suffered and caused suffering. He's an angel, but his influence works out badly as often as it works out well. Some care too much, and some not enough. Some make efforts, and some take no responsibility. But whatever we do, we don't seem to do well.' Turning to Stephen, she saw with relief that he was not angered, and her relief made her cringe inwardly.

Attending minutely, yet with deep self-absorption, Stephen said, 'You don't have to look beyond the morning paper. But the disillusionment's more personal than that. Isn't it?'

'So there is something wrong,' Zoe sighed, as though he were the final authority. 'Yes, it's personal, but it's all connected, too. I've always had such faith, such a lot of faith in—but it was all a mistake. Like all the rest. We were a mistake.'

The strap of her sandal was twisted. Sighing again, she leaned down to straighten it, and heard Stephen say, 'You'll go, then?'

'Yes.'

Lily called them from the top of the garden and came wandering down. 'I've spoken to the girls in London. Great reconciliations! I'm flying over next week, or the instant I can get my passport.'

'I thought only Russell had come to see us.' Zoe kissed her and took her hand, and Stephen made room for her on the wall. 'Come and sit down here in the middle.'

'We were up all night talking,' Lily said energetically. 'Booking calls to the girls. The upshot is—I'm off indefinitely. I wanted a suitable father for my children and picked Russell. Your mother and father liked me, Zo. (Because of tennis, I think.) He was away all those years. When he came home, I was the girl he knew. He was quite defenceless. If he hadn't come back, I'd have found someone else of good intelligence and I'd have been equally happy, as long as we'd had children.

'I know, according to all the rules, I ought to put up some sort of struggle out of sheer possessiveness. If it had happened while the girls were here, it might have been different. But it's been fairly obvious since they went away how much they mattered to me. Anna's not like that. He's more to her than any man could be to me. And she never has found anyone to take his place.'

Behind her head, Stephen's and Zoe's eyes met in a complex look that acknowledged their own parting, while wondering at Lily's justice and calm. Hesitantly, Zoe said, 'You're very generous and fair.'

Lily started to cry. 'Am I? I'm not! I'm not! You didn't hear what I said last night. I hate them! I hate them!' She started to search herself for a handkerchief, and as though to keep her in countenance, the others felt themselves over, too. Stephen produced one. A few seconds later, Lily gave a last wrenching sob and was still. Zoe put an arm across her shoulders.

'Hell and damn! I didn't mean to do that. I got all dressed up and made up. I was going to put on a brave show.'

'You have. You did. You're terrific,' she was assured.

'I don't really hate them. I was going away, anyway. Now, I'll stay longer. Because I not only have my girls in London, but my sisters are in England, too.' Her voice had taken on a hushed, religious note. 'We're very close.'

No one commented.

Much more briskly, Lily added, 'And I'm very keen to get on with some work.'

Warding off Lily's attempts to return his handkerchief, Stephen asked, 'What's happening about Russell and Anna? I suppose I shouldn't ask.'

'Why not?' She looked straight ahead. Her voice was hard. 'They're going to be extremely happy. How could I have been so dense? It's the real thing. If you weren't involved, the way I am, you could probably think it all quite splendid, quite beautiful. I can't rise to that. Damn their eyes! Now I'll remove myself and we'll arrange a divorce and true love can have its way.

'I'd better go before I start to be very unpleasant. You and I are supposed to see the solicitor tomorrow, Zo. I'll ring you later today. Russell's going to a hotel for a couple of weeks. He could have stayed, but it's better not. The brave show might wear thin. Don't come with me. No farewells.'

Helpless to help, forbidden to speak, they watched her walk away.

'*Lily*...' Zoe called. 'Let's drive you home. One of us...' She looked at Stephen. 'Please.'

Turning, Lily held her head at an angle of assent and gratitude. Relieved to do her the least service, Zoe and Stephen walked with her up to the garage through the garden.

'I'd sink into the sand if I walked along the beach. We brought the car, but Russell needs it.' Parting, she said, to explain and console, 'I felt the other so much, I feel this less. Don't be sad.'

Glancing at Stephen, Zoe could only shake her head and try to smile, leaving Lily to make what she could of it. So everything's over and beginning, she thought, when they had driven off and she was sitting on the sun-warmed steps of the verandah. But I am sad for her. For him, for myself, the others. Yet even while she told herself so, grief and gladness and acceptance and hope mingled in her, and the mingling was like the flight of skylarks—as high and light.

What an effort to change, she thought, hardly daring yet to notice the spontaneous, given changes taking place in herself. Anna went to the very door of death to make change possible, and then later, accidentally, it altered everyone. Stephen's theory that having invested time you would be disinclined to consider it wasted was one way of seeing. When you put your hand to the plough, you don't turn back—or some such thing. Implying: someone with my sterling character would never change her mind. (Perseverance, good my lord, keeps honour bright!) But you could also say: someone with my rigid character could never admit to having been wrong. Or you might see the time as creative. Let it have been so for them, too!

What a slow learner, she thought, slowly rising. Still, the day was lovely. And now she could move on.